THEY DIDN'T KNOW

PAM EATON

COOPER AVE PRESS

For Harmony -
I miss you so much. I think about you all the time. I wish you had
stayed. This life isn't the same without you in it.

CONTENTS

1

I THOUGHT I KNEW WHAT HELL WAS: THE SCORCHING TEMPERATURES of a Phoenix summer; moving to a Connecticut beach house in the dead of winter; the weeks spent in a mental health facility. But now—hell is being trapped here on this couch, with a plastic smile on my face, listening to my mom wax poetic about her motivational posters. Hell is the place I've been trapped in for the past eight months. Some days I'm waiting for the flames to rise up and consume me, and some days I can feel the thick coat of ash on my tongue. Some days...some days I don't know why I bother to stay.

"What about this one, Tori?" my mom asks. She turns toward me, hugging a frame to her chest, a fragile hope shining in her eyes.

I put down the book I'm supposed to be reading for my new school and look at the poster from my spot on the couch.

You have to look through the rain to see the rainbow.

"Uh—"

"It's true, you know. The bad days will pass," she says, but it seems like she's trying to convince herself of that more than me.

She stares at the frame and gives it a small nod. And this is why I have to stay. I can't crush her any more than I have. Some days the pressure of trying to keep it all together makes me want to let the flames devour me. But every day I wake up.

She taps a finger to her lips. "I think I'll put this one in the stairwell."

This is the fifth poster she's brought out. Who comes up with these phrases? Is there some guy out there that trolls retirement homes looking for sage wisdom or confusing anecdotes on life? I overheard her telling my dad that hanging these up around the house is going to change everything. I don't think looking at a sign that says "Tomorrow is a new day" is going to make me forget what I tried to do last year.

"I'm going to get some fresh air," I tell her, rising from the couch.

"Sure, sure," she says, looking at her next poster. "Grab a coat," she calls as I leave her to her motivational quotes and make my way to the back door in the kitchen. I've done my mandatory hour of sitting in Mom's presence. I need out. I grab my jacket and throw on some shoes.

I push open the storm door and a freezing wind lashes at my face. It somehow finds every gap in my clothing and pierces my skin. I let the sting of the cold air envelop me as I move across the yard. It steals my breath and yet makes me feel a little bit more alive.

The house looms above me. Maybe in my other life I would have called it cute with its blue wood siding and flower box-lined, white-trimmed windows. Mom said the front yard will be bursting with hydrangeas and lilacs come late spring. It's nothing like home though. There are no palm trees, no desert landscaping filled with rocks and cacti. None of the houses here have stucco walls or scorpions—the no scorpions part is a plus if I'm being honest with myself. Everything feels off, but that's been a constant for a while now. We moved to where my mom grew up for a fresh start, but I still haven't figured out how my parents think moving across the country is going to accomplish that. Either way, this whole "Fix Tori" project has landed me on this freezing cold, desolate beach at our new home.

I move through the small yard toward the sand bordering it, letting the stab of icy wind rip through me. I try to take a deep breath, but the air is so cold that it feels like needles slicing at my lungs. I look back from my spot near the water and sure enough, Mom is in the kitchen hanging another poster.

I exhale a white cloud. *It makes her happy; just let her do it.*

I've learned the hard way not to comment about those posters around her. The last time I did it sent her into hysterical tears, which in turn led to disappointed and concerned looks from my dad. The last thing I want is to be locked up in a mental health facility, rooming with some girl who steals the hair from my brush and chants words in Latin late at night. Again.

And as much as I want to tell her that the only useful thing about those posters is the glass, I rein in that dark humor. Because I know it would be a one-way ticket back to my own personal Bedlam.

The reminder of *that night* makes me rub at the scars under the leather cuffs on my wrists. I almost got the pain to stop, and then my mom found me. Now here I am, broken, standing on frozen sea foam outside our new home.

I look out at the endless stretch of water, and I feel...

Nothing.

Nothing but a pit in my heart that I can't figure out how to fill. And most days, I don't know if I want to.

* * *

"Tori! Kris is here with Danielle," my mom yells, jolting me back to reality.

I have no clue how long I've been standing here, but it's been long enough that I've lost feeling in my toes. I take a deep breath and turn around slowly, looking at the visitors in the kitchen. My shoulders fall at seeing my mom's friend Kris. I trudge the short distance back to the house, dreading this.

The overwhelming smell of Windex greets me as I enter the kitchen. Guess Mom went a little overboard with cleaning those frames. Kris watches me as I struggle to get my fingers to move and untie my shoes.

I haven't seen my mom's best friend in five years. She really hasn't changed much. She still has the same haircut like those memes making fun of a lady asking to speak to a manager. Her clothes scream soccer mom, which is weird because I've seen pictures of them from high school, and they were popular cheer-leaders. Time could have been kind, but it's like Kris slapped it and said no. Regardless, she knows all about last summer. And her eyes track my movements, like she thinks at any moment I'll throw a chair across the room or grab a sharp object.

Or maybe she's afraid I'll be a bad influence on her daughter, Danielle.

"Hey guys," I say, giving an awkward wave to both of them.

"Hello, Victoria," Kris says in a weird, slow voice. "How are you?"

What is with *that* voice? I blink a few times, trying to see if she's seriously talking to me like I suddenly can't understand English. Apparently, she is. All right.

"Fine," I say.

She makes a humming noise like she doesn't believe me. "You remember Danielle," she says, pointing at her daughter sitting at the table. It's been five years since I last saw Dani in person, and a year since we exchanged messages on Instagram before I deleted all my social media accounts.

"Why is she talking to me like I suffered brain damage?" I ask my mom in a whisper, which is pointless since our kitchen isn't that big and I know everyone heard me.

"Victoria Adams," Mom says my name on a harsh gasp, while Kris looks like she's sucked on a lemon.

"Hey, Tori," Dani butts in, trying to contain her laughter but failing miserably.

Dani is no longer the stick-thin eleven-year-old we both used to be. Now she looks like she could pass for a Kardashian with those curves. Apparently, my body didn't get that memo. She gets out of her chair and wraps me in a tight hug. Everything in me seizes at her touch. We used to hug like this all the time, but just like her boobs have changed, so has my fondness for human contact. Thankfully the hug is over as quickly as it began. "I'm so excited you guys moved here," Dani says. "And don't worry, I'll totally take care of you at school."

School. One word, but it sends my heart racing. Last semester I did school online. But my parents weren't okay with that option when we moved here.

"Can't wait to be the new girl," I say.

"I'm sure they'll hardly notice a new student," Mom says, trying to be helpful.

"They'll notice," Kris mutters, eyes looking at my wrists.

Everyone turns to look at her. She visibly flinches like she just realizes she said that out loud. "I mean, you're a pretty girl, of course they'll notice," she stammers out.

Real nice, Kris.

"You're starting tomorrow, right?" Dani asks, dragging my attention away from her noticeably nervous, sweating mom.

"Yeah," I answer on a sigh.

"Good. I'll pick you up so we can go together." Her body vibrates with excitement, and I take a small step back.

I nod, because what am I going to do? Tell her no? Or say: sorry, I'd rather not be alone with you so you can ask me fifty million questions? I know it's normal for someone to want to know what happened, but that doesn't mean I have to spell it out for them. It makes my heart squeeze in agony to imagine what it would be like to actually say the words out loud. Besides, she wouldn't get it.

"Oh, that would be wonderful, Danielle! I'm so glad you asked," my mom pipes in.

I know my mom thinks that if I just fall back into school and hang around people, it's going to help, but how do I tell her that I can feel alone in a crowded room? How do I explain that it doesn't matter how nice these kids are to me because it won't fix the broken things within me? There is no miracle cure.

Kris stands from the table and grabs her purse, inching toward the living room. "Well, we just wanted to stop by, but we've got errands to run."

She tries to sound apologetic, but we all saw her eyeing me the entire time. I mean, come on, it's not like I decided to dye my hair pitch black and wear black lipstick. And even if I did, who cares? I'm not out back burning sacrificial lambs or anything.

I look down at myself. I *do* wear baggier clothes and hardly any makeup. But I want to blend in, not stick out.

My mom walks Kris to the door, but Dani hangs back a bit. "You don't have to give me a ride to school," I whisper so my mom doesn't overhear.

She waves away my comment. "I want to. We used to be super close. I still consider you one of my good friends." She chews on her bottom lip. "And don't worry, I won't tell anyone about"—she gestures toward my wrists—"that."

My stomach lurches. My hands tremble, so I tuck them behind my back. Of course she knows I tried to kill myself. Granted she doesn't know why—not even my parents know why—but her bringing it up feels like a punch to the gut. "Thanks," I somehow manage to squeeze out between my pinched lips.

"Here," she says, taking out her phone and handing it to me. "Put your number in here and I'll text you to let you know when I'll pick you up."

With still-shaking hands, I take her phone and type my number in. As I start to hand it back, the close-up picture of her and some guy on her lock screen snags my attention. He's gorgeous, with dark brown curls in need of a cut, bright blue eyes, and an infectious smile. He's exactly the type of guy I used to go for, until *him*. I shudder at the mere thought of him, but at least I don't feel the need to throw up. Progress.

Dani follows my gaze, and I'm hoping she doesn't notice how stark white my hand is from gripping her phone so hard. "Oh, that's my best friend, Nick. Isn't he hot?"

I all but shove her phone back to her. "Yeah. Sure. Could use a haircut."

Her smile becomes a little dreamy. "Yeah, but I like it."

Just a best friend? "All right. Well, text me." I start walking to the door in the hopes that she'll follow.

She trails after me but stops halfway out the front door and looks at me with a hopeful smile. "You know, if you ever want to hang out or something you can come out with me and my friends."

I rock back on my heels. There's a part of me that wants to jump at the chance of some sort of normalcy. There are days when I crave it. But the churning pit in my stomach holds me back every time. "I'll let you know." There. That was a very neutral and non-committal answer.

With one last wave she leaves me standing at the door, having no idea that my hands are still clenched or that beads of sweat are slowly trailing down my back.

"That's so thoughtful of Danielle to pick you up for school," my mom says from behind me.

"Yeah," I say, not elaborating.

"Do you want help picking out an outfit for tomorrow?" she asks, sounding hopeful.

I slowly turn and face her, knowing my face is contorted in horror. "Uh...no, I think I've got that covered, Mom."

Her shoulders slump a little and I can't figure out why. She hasn't dressed me since the first grade. And I've got no clue what she'd try to get me to wear. But I'll stick with my standard look lately: invisible. "Oh, okay. Well, I'm going to go figure out dinner. Dad should be home from work soon."

She trudges back to the kitchen, her body slumped in defeat, and I want to scream because I somehow managed to hurt her feelings, again.

I pull at the roots of my hair. I can't keep doing this. I'm going crazy walking on eggshells around her. Well, more crazy than usual.

2

I park my butt by the front window, but I kind of wish I hadn't because now I'm stuck staring at my own reflection. Baggy boyfriend jeans, grey long-sleeved shirt that covers *everything*, and my trusty black hoodie with the thumb holes that helps hide my leather cuffs. The only good thing about living in Connecticut: it stays colder longer than it does in Arizona, allowing me to wear layers without questioning looks.

A car horn honks, dragging my eyes from the dreary site. Dani waves from the driver's seat. I lean forward and squint. My heart stutters. She's not alone. There's a guy sitting next to her. A burning starts underneath my leather cuffs and I rub them against my jeans. When she texted me yesterday, she didn't say anything about driving someone else. I lick my lips and Dani honks again and waves. I blink. Crap, they can totally see me standing in the window like a creeper. I shove my beanie on my head and pull my long brown hair forward.

"I'm leaving," I yell to my mom.

She walks out of the kitchen with a large, hopeful smile and her hands clasped in front of her. "Have a good day, baby. You're coming straight home after school, right?"

My forehead furrows. "Where else would I go?"

She gives a little shrug. "Well, you might make some friends today…"

I won't give her false hope. It's not good for either of us. For just a moment I let my walls down so she can see what lurks behind my eyes. So she'll see that I won't be going anywhere today with new friends. And I give her that quick glimpse of how miserable I really am.

I turn without waiting to see her reaction, but that doesn't mean I don't hear her pain-filled gasp. I walk out the door without another word.

I trudge toward the car, my mood already souring, and notice the guy in the front seat is Nick, the guy from Dani's phone. He's got a huge grin on his face and laughs at something Dani says. A pang of longing hits my chest. I can't remember the last time I laughed like that.

I slide into the backseat and curl up against the door. Dani turns around in her seat, her eyes bright and her smile huge. "Tori, meet Nick Janus; Nick, I'd like you to meet Tori."

"Hey," Nick says, turning to look at me with friendly eyes.

I give a little wave and then pull my hoodie tight around me. He bites his lip and glances at Dani. "Sooo, let's head to school," she says in a false-cheery voice.

As she backs out, Nick doesn't turn back around to the front, instead he still stares at me. His eyes travel from my beanie and down to the holes where my thumbs are sticking out of my hoodie's sleeves. I shift in my seat.

"You know, my best friend Zack used to live in your house," he tells me.

I raise my eyebrows and shrug. He tilts his head, studying me some more. "You don't talk much," he states like he knows me.

I stare back at him for a second and then look out the window. I'm being totally rude, but I haven't been this close to another guy besides my dad in a long time. Even if I wanted to, I can't open my mouth and talk to him. I'm too busy trying to take deep breaths and get my hands to stop shaking. I don't know why I let my parents talk me into going back to school. I can't sit in a car with a guy without having a full-blown panic attack. How the hell am I going to handle an entire day at school with hundreds of them?

I catch Dani's frown in the mirror. I know I seemed fine the other day and now I'm mute, but I was with people I knew then. Nick taps the seat and I drag my eyes back to his face. "Don't worry; I'll have you talking to me in no time. People, especially women, can't resist talking with me." His voice is totally serious, but his eyes are alight with humor.

I shake my head, scoffing a little at how cocky he sounds.

"Dani! Did you hear that? I got her to make a noise. Progress, I say! Progress!" He punches the air.

My body relaxes a little and I let my arms fall to my sides instead of tight across my chest.

"Yeah," Nick continues. "So, my best friend Zack used to live there until his parents moved and made him enroll in some crazy military school. Totally random, and wherever the school is, they're living off the land or something like that. No internet or phones. I couldn't do it."

I stare back at him, not knowing if he's expecting a response from me regarding his best friend whose parents made him abandon civilization. "I miss him," he says more to himself than anyone else, but he shakes himself out of it. "Anyways, I live two doors down from you, so if you ever decide to break this vow of silence, come over and hang out."

I give him nothing. Go to a guy's house? No way; never again. I start to feel my body tighten again at the thought, but thank goodness we're pulling into the school a moment later.

Dani parks and we all climb out. Nick waves at someone. "Thanks for the lift, Dani. And I'll see you guys later," he says, and jogs over to a truck full of guys.

"Hey, what's with the silent routine?" Dani asks.

I turn away from watching Nick and look at her face all scrunched up. "Nothing, just really tired and fought with my mom right before I walked out the door." I mean, I'm not *really* lying, but that response will have to work.

She studies me for a moment. "Okay. Do you want me to show you the way to the office?"

I let out a slow breath. If I don't learn to fake being better, she's going to catch on that I'm not, in fact, better. And I'd rather keep people ignorant on what's really running through my brain. "Yeah, that'd be great. Thanks."

The feel of eyes fixed on me causes me to pause. I try to sneak a look over my shoulder at the direction it's coming from. Nick and the guys he's standing with are all watching me. He gives me a huge, cheesy wink. I shake my head and catch up to Dani. We walk up the steps and head toward the glass front doors of Saybrooke High School.

As soon as we're inside I hug my arms around my middle. My school back in Arizona had over three thousand kids in it, making it easier to disappear into a crowd. Not here though, because everyone's eyes hit me as I make my way down the hall with Dani. She walks with purpose, head up, waving at everyone that greets her. Which is almost everyone. Of course she's popular. But what makes my stomach turn a bit is all the whispers that start as soon as they realize I'm walking with her. The fact that I'm new at this tiny school makes me the hottest gossip, and add in the fact I'm with Dani just fuels it even more. Awesome.

We stop in front of the office door. "I'll wait out here for you while you grab your schedule," Dani says, looking up and down the hall.

"Wish me luck," I tell her. I take a deep breath and open the door.

* * *

Auto shop? I close my eyes and open them again to make sure. Nope, still there. I look back up at the secretary, Ms. Clapman. "Excuse me, this can't be right."

She takes a deep breath, like *I'm* getting on her nerves. She better take a deeper breath though, because if this doesn't get changed, I'm going to freak out. "What appears to be the problem?"

Does she really have to use that tone? The first bell hasn't even rung—how is she already so annoyed today? Maybe she's always like this.

"I never signed up for auto shop. I don't even know how to drive a car, never mind work on one." I tap my finger against the counter. She clears her throat and looks pointedly at my hand until I stop tapping. I can tell she doesn't understand why I'm upset about *this* class. I can't go in there.

She purses her cracked red lips. "Well, this is all that's available for electives. If you want to pass your junior year, you have to take it."

My lungs squeeze painfully in my chest. This has to change. "Is there anyone I can talk to and fix this?" My voice reeks of desperation, and I can only imagine how much my face matches my voice.

I fail miserably at getting her sympathy, because she turns back to her computer, totally dismissing me. "You could try talking to a counselor, but they have no openings until next week." She reaches a hand back and taps a clipboard. I pounce on it like the lifeline it is, writing my name and new student ID on the signup sheet.

I look back down at my schedule, my heart beating a crazy

rhythm. *I can do this. I can do this.* Maybe if I keep telling myself that, it'll come true?

Who am I kidding? I can't do this.

I trudge back out into the hallway, defeated, and find Dani talking with a group of girls. I step up beside her, catching her attention. "Give me your schedule," she says, and then proceeds to rip it out of my hand.

As she reads over it, the three other girls stare at me. I give a pathetic wave.

All three of them are beautiful. And they look exactly like the type of girls I used to hang out with at my old school.

Dani's head pops up from reading. "Oh yeah, sorry guys. This is my friend Tori I was telling you about that lives in Zack's old house. Tori, this is Regina, Gretchen, and Britney."

Those have got to be the most cliché popular girls' names ever, not to mention this is like the line-up from *Mean Girls*. Almost. Just missing Karen; then again, I'm no Cady.

Regina stands a little taller than my own five-foot-six frame. Her long, sleek black hair drapes artfully over one shoulder. She's got amazing cat-like eyes, deep brown skin, and a body most girls would die for. Gretchen, on the other hand, looks like a little pixie that could fit in my pocket, but her smile is large and warm. Her blonde hair falls in waves nearly to the small of her back. Britney gives me pause at the look on her face. Her deep brown eyes barely conceal a sadness that I know all too well.

"So, we have English and lunch together," Dani says, making my eyes snap back to her.

I could sink to the floor with relief. Thank goodness I have at least one class with her, and I won't be the weird new girl sitting by herself at lunch. Even if I don't want to be here, being the loner at lunch sucks.

The bell blares above our heads. "That's only the warning

bell," Dani instructs. "Regina has homeroom with you, so go with her."

Regina looks at me with an extremely fake smile, giving my clothes a once-over. "Uh... sure. Just follow me."

I have the sudden urge to point out that my jeans are name brand and that I have in fact showered today, but I don't bother. Let her think what she wants. I pull my water bottle from my bag and take a sip before following Regina.

"Oh, and don't worry, Tori's not one of those anti-social girls who's going to carve your name into a voodoo doll or anything," Dani tells them.

I cough, choking on my drink. I'm sure I look like I'm having a seizure now with water dribbling down my chin. It's a really nice touch. "Umm, thanks for that raving review," I say, wiping my face.

"Well, right now you have this aversion to colors and form-fitting clothes going on," Dani says, gesturing to my outfit, and Gretchen giggles from beside her.

"I'm going for comfort," I say.

"Sure," she says, giving me a reassuring smile.

Apparently, our exchange satisfies Regina, because she grabs my sleeve and throws me a genuine smile. "Let's get going to homeroom."

I take a deep breath. Here goes nothing.

3

My plan for hiding in the back of the class, away from everyone, is immediately shredded as Regina takes me to the center of the room. We also happen to be some of the last to arrive, so everyone stares as we claim a couple of empty seats.

Here's one of the problems with being a new student and entering with a popular girl. Lately, I wouldn't be given a second glance with how I dress and how I try to blend into the background. But since I didn't scurry into the back of the room like my original plan, and instead walked in with Regina, I'm totally looked over. By everyone.

I'm sure most of them are trying to figure out why Regina is coming into class with *me*. Maybe they think I'm her charity case? Who knows? But right now, I wish I could disappear.

"Guys, this is Tori," Regina tells the group around us. "She's new here and friends with Dani. Oh, and she lives in Zack's old house."

Is this how I'm going to be labeled from now on: the girl that lives in Zack's old house?

16

I give a lame little wave—again— and what follows is a chorus of "heys" and head-nods.

Regina immediately starts doing something on her phone, so I face forward and wait for the inevitable. I've never been the new kid at school, but if television is actually right for once, I'm going to have to introduce myself all day. I don't know why I have to do this. I'm not going to be friends with everyone in this room, so why do they have to put me on display? Maybe if I were the type that wanted to be class president or something, I would want everyone to know me, but any desire for that has long vanished.

As the second bell rings, in walks Nick. He says hi to everyone that greets him, and he adds in the complicated hand-slap thing that guys always do. His eyes land on me and his face breaks out into a huge smile. I sink down into my seat in a futile attempt to hide. "New neighbor," he says as he walks my way.

He has to be the happiest person I've ever encountered.

"You've met Tori?" Regina asks, looking between us.

"Oh yeah, we go *way* back," he tells her.

She looks over at me expectantly, like I've kept this huge secret from her.

I wait for Nick to explain, but he doesn't. "Dani drove us both to school today," I tell her.

"Way to rat me out," Nick whisper-shouts.

He sits in the empty seat in front of me and immediately turns around. I look down and intently study my fingernails. I know he's looking at me, probably smiling. What is with this guy? And then I feel it, the moment he wants to ask me a question. Right as I see his mouth open to ask something I probably don't want to answer, our homeroom teacher walks in and calls our attention.

Nick turns forward and I take a deep breath.

"We have a new student today, Victoria Adams," my home-room teacher, Mr. Knell, announces.

Everyone turns to look at me. And it's super uncomfortable. After trying to stay under the radar for the past year, having all these people watching me…it feels invasive. It feels like they know I'm a fraud.

"Victoria, please come up here and introduce yourself," Mr. Knell says to me.

Fantastic. Stupid TV shows were right.

I slide out of my seat and keep my eyes on the whiteboard as I walk to the front of the room. This is awful. I should be used to this—being the center of attention—I was on varsity cheer at my old school. But that was before. Now, I want to be ignored, not paraded around. I get to the front and turn slowly. Too many eyes examine me. Nick gives me a big smile with a thumbs-up. A small part of me wants to laugh, but it's not enough. I fix my eyes on a spot over Regina's shoulder. "Hi. I'm Tori."

I make to move back to my seat, but Mr. Knell stops me. "Well, Tori, tell us something about yourself." Why won't he let me go back to my seat? Sadistic torturer.

I rub at the cuffs on my wrist. "Umm. I just moved here from Arizona."

A stretch of silence ensues when I don't say anything else. Mr. Knell clears his throat when the silence stretches too long. "Okay… well, we're glad you're here, Tori."

I walk back to my seat, much faster than when I left it a moment ago. "Maybe she's shy," I hear someone whisper, but I don't acknowledge it and keep moving back to my chair.

I stiffly sink back into my seat and pin my eyes on the whiteboard as Mr. Knell gives the morning announcements. How the hell am I supposed to go through a whole day of the staring, the endless questions, the ridiculous amount of energy to just *be*? This was such a mistake. I should have just kept doing school online.

* * *

"How's being the new girl?" Britney asks me as she takes the seat next to mine in the back of the room of our math class. Guess I'm not hiding during this hour, either.

I study her face, looking for sarcasm, but all I see is genuine concern. "It sucks," I tell her.

She smiles and her face transforms from pretty into stunning. "It's a small school. Nothing really exciting happens here." Her face falls for a minute. "Except for when people move suddenly."

"Like that Zack guy?" I ask.

She glances away. "Yeah."

I feel like I should apologize or something for moving into Zack's house, or maybe pat her shoulder. I'm so bad at this comforting people thing now. "You must miss him" is what I opt for. Because from how she looks, it's obvious.

She nods and then takes a deep breath, seeming to shake herself out of it. "Anyways, this class is pretty easy."

It's hard to miss her changing the subject. So I roll with it, dropping the subject of Zack. "Algebra and me are not friends," I tell her in all honesty, making her laugh and taking a little of the sadness out of her eyes.

"Well, I can help you study sometime. Just let me know," she says with a small smile.

She seems like a genuinely nice person, and for that I'm grateful. The thought of only being friends with Dani is exhausting. She always has some drama going on, but Britney seems different. Maybe a little lost like me.

4

I drop my lunch tray in front of Dani and her friends. "I'm thinking someone needs to fill me in on this Zack guy. It's been a long day of 'oooh, she lives in Zack's house'," I tell the group of girls.

Dani leans forward, looking all too eager to fill me in. "From what Nick said, Zack's parents found out he was doing drugs again. So they shipped him off to some military wilderness school or something. And Nick didn't even get to say goodbye to his best friend. Weird, right?"

"Yeah, but why did his parents move so suddenly?" I ask. "It's kind of random."

"They're all about appearances," Britney says in a somber voice. "I don't think his mom could handle all the stares. Everyone knows Zack; everybody loves him. I'm guessing they didn't want to explain that he's got some demons."

Dani lifts a brow at me, but I ignore it. I wonder how long till everyone knows why *we* moved here. I don't have any plans on telling anyone here, but it only takes one person saying something for word to spread. Plus, my parents didn't move to keep everyone from knowing in Arizona. They already knew what I did.

Britney stands from the table. "I'll be back," she says, and hurries in the direction of the cafeteria's door.

Gretchen gets up and rushes after her. I look between Dani and Regina, a question plain on my face.

"Britney and Zack used to date," Dani fills me in. "They were on and off all the time. And when his family up and moved him without a word, they had just gone through a nasty fight. She hasn't heard from him in like months."

I watch Britney walk through the door, Gretchen trailing behind her. "That sucks."

"Yeah, especially because she really loves him," Regina adds in.

I cringe. Definitely sucks for her.

My breath slows as two girls I haven't met approach the table, both wearing cheerleading outfits. An image of me walking the halls on game day in my cheer clothes flashes in front of me. I close my eyes and give my head a little shake.

"Hey Melanie, Cara," Dani greets them. "Come meet Tori."

They plop down across from us. Melanie's dark curls bounce around her face as gives me a big smile. Her royal-blue uniform stands out against her dark skin. It's a beautiful combination. Cara, on the other hand, doesn't even spare me a glance. She tucks a piece of blonde hair behind her ear and looks around the room. I guess it was too much to hope that *all* of Dani's friends would be cool with me.

"Game day?" I ask.

"Yeah," Melanie says. "The boys' basketball team is at home tonight."

"Tori's a cheerleader," Dani pipes in, an encouraging smile on her face. "You should see her stunts—they're amazing."

Everyone at the table looks at my outfit again. "Really?" Regina asks dubiously.

"I don't cheer anymore," I throw in before anyone gets an idea about me joining the squad.

"Oh, that's too bad. We would have loved to have you on the team," Cara says with a fake pout.

"Maybe next year," I say, but there's no way I'll be cheering again.

"So, what class do you have next?" Regina asks, thankfully breaking the awkwardness. Because I can feel the questions these girls have about me wanting to break loose.

Bless her for changing the subject, but it's just going to get awkward again. "Auto shop."

All the girls stop whatever they were doing and stare at me like I just said I was going to run through the school naked. "You're taking auto shop?" Melanie asks, looking horrified.

"It was the only elective left, and I need one." Why I'm defending this, I have no clue. But it's not like I'm willingly stepping into that class.

"At least there are some hot guys in there," Cara adds, sounding somewhat jealous.

"I guess there's that," I say, but she definitely doesn't pick up on the sarcasm in my voice.

"Nick's in there, you can sit with him," Dani tells me.

I nod, not bothering to answer, because I could care less who's in that class. I don't plan on staying in it for long.

* * *

The door to auto class looms in front of me. I still have time. I could skip class. No one would notice. Not sure anyone would care. I start to turn when the door is thrown open and a burly-looking lumberjack stands on the other side. "Welcome," he bellows.

This is my teacher? My body locks, because this guy is massive. His smile is huge, his hands are like the size of my head, and I'm not sure if I could outrun him. My chest tightens. Air. I need air.

His smile falls a bit as he studies me.

"Come on in," he says a lot more gently, stepping a good distance back.

Pretend this is just like walking into English. Except this isn't English or even art class. Because if it was, I'd probably only get a fleeting glance. But stick a female into an all-male auto shop, might as well have a flashing neon sign above my head. Every guy stares at me as I slowly shuffle into the room, and it's taking everything in me not to turn around and run like hell.

I reach down and rub at the leather cuff on my left wrist.

"And who are you?" lumberjack guy asks.

My eyes dart between him and the rest of the class. Okay, changed my mind. I can't do this.

He shifts and stands in front of me, blocking out the class. A sliver of tension leaves me. At least now I'm not on display for all those guys. I take as big a breath as I can, considering it feels like someone is sitting on my chest. "I'm—" My voice cracks and I have to clear my throat a few times. I can do this. "I'm Tori Adams."

"Hello, Tori, I'm Mr. Jackelowitz." I'm sorry, what did he just say? "But you can call me Mr. Jack."

A hysterical laugh starts to bubble up in my throat, but I swallow it down. Of course he would be Mr. Jack, where the heck is his ax? He's already got the plaid shirt.

"So, Tori, what can I do for you?" he asks.

I pull out the crumbled schedule from my back pocket and hand it to him. His bushy eyebrows reach his hairline. "You're signed up for auto shop?"

He frowns down at me, clearly confused. *You and me both,*

lumberjack. "I needed an elective and this was all that's left," I say with a shrug.

He scratches his scruffy cheek and looks at my schedule for a moment longer. "Probably should check my email more often. Well, that's okay, you're more than welcome here. Why don't you go find an empty seat?"

I scan the room, looking at the tables filled with guys.

"Over here, Tori." I slowly turn at the sound of Nick's voice. "You can come sit with us."

He's at a table with two other huge guys. One of them gives me a top-to-toe scan and it makes my skin crawl. No way, not going to happen. So I do the totally rude thing and make my way to the table near the door with the loner guy of the class. I don't want to sit here, but this kid looks more interested in World of Warcraft than me.

As I sit, I hear one of the guys at Nick's table snicker. "She just ignored you," he says, laughing.

"It's because you smell, Jackson, that's why," Nick says back.

"All right, guys—oh sorry, and lady—settle down," Mr. Jack booms. "Today we're going to pair up to work on the assignment we talked about. Remember, this is worth half of your grade."

What?

I try to grab the teacher's attention with my eyes, but he's too busy passing out papers. As he gets closer, I clear my throat, loudly.

"Yes, Tori?" he asks, putting a paper in front of me.

"I don't know what you're talking about."

"Oh, that's right. Well, hmm..." He plants his large hands on his hips and looks around the room.

We're starting to draw attention, and little by little I sink lower into my seat. "She can partner with me." Nick pops up next to me.

"That's a great idea," Mr. Jack says, his thunderous voice nearly crippling my eardrums.

Nick shrugs. "Zack was going to be my partner, but with him gone, Tori can fill in." There's a hint of sadness to his tone.

Mr. Jack claps him on the shoulder, and Nick grimaces. Can't blame him—I probably would have fallen to the floor. "Perfect. Here why don't you sit down and explain to her what we'll be doing."

He walks off, leaving us alone. Well, loner guy is there too, but he quickly gets up from his seat and moves across the room to his partner. I stare over Nick's shoulder, waiting for him to fill me in. "I'm guessing you didn't plan to take this class," he says, sitting in the seat next to me.

"Was definitely *not* my first choice of classes."

"That's okay, we'll have fun doing this project."

I don't know if he's trying to convince himself or me, because I know *nothing* about cars.

"Luckily, Zack and I were already thinking of what we could do." There's that sadness again.

"You miss him, huh?" The question comes flying out before I can stop it, surprising both of us.

"Of course—he's my best friend," he says like it's the most obvious thing in the world.

I can't remember what that's like anymore—having a best friend. And wow, that's a super depressing thought. Even more, I don't think there's anyone that I'd miss as much as Nick misses Zack.

"Anyways, we already started working on rebuilding an engine," he says.

Say what? Rebuilding an engine? Guess I'm about to burst his bubble. I lean on the table. "Can I be honest with you?"

"Always."

"I can put gas in a car, but that's about it. I have no idea how much help I'm going to be on this project." I may not want to take this class, but I definitely don't want to fail it.

Maybe I can convince Mr. Jack to let me do something else, or hopefully when I see the school counselor, she'll get me out of this nightmare.

"It'll be fine. I'll show you what to do," Nick says, sounding a lot more assured than I am. He has way too much confidence about this.

What also takes me by surprise is the ease I'm finding when I talk with him. Don't get me wrong, he still puts me on edge, but I don't want to run for the door. When's the last time I held a conversation with a guy this long?

He reaches across me for the sheet of instructions and my whole body flinches. His eyes dart to mine. So much for that ease I was just feeling a second ago.

Please don't say anything.

He hesitates for a second and then grabs the paper and leans back in his seat. "This shows us the guidelines for the project."

The relief coursing through my system is palpable. But I have no clue how we're going to work on this together. He gets too close and I freak out. And I'm assuming we're going to get *real* close working on a car engine.

I try taking deep breaths, but as he rambles on about the project, I'm trying to figure a way out of it. This is the last straw. I have to drop this class.

I have to drop this class.

I *have* to drop this class.

5

———————

"Sooo, how was auto shop?" Dani asks me as I plop in a seat next to her. Thank goodness we have English together.

"Awesome," I groan.

She laughs. "You don't have to make it sound like a death sentence."

"It kind of is, though. I'm the only girl in there. When I walked in, you would have thought those guys had never seen a female before."

She gets a dreamy look on her face. "I'll trade with you. I would *love* to be in a class with all guys."

I'm sure she would.

"I would trade with you in a heartbeat if I could," I tell her in all seriousness.

"Oh, come on, it wasn't that bad," Nick says from the desk next to me.

My head whips to the left. This guy just keeps popping up out of nowhere.

"Well, with you in it, Nick, it's probably the best class," Dani says in a flirty tone, but Nick just laughs her off.

"Only because you'd make me do all the work, Dani. And I would, because that's what friends do. Not to mention I refuse to fail auto shop."

Dani's face drops a little at the friend comment, but she quickly covers it with a bright smile. And it's like Nick doesn't even register it. Wow, how does he not realize that she totally likes him?

"You really hate the class?" he asks me.

I shift in my chair. "It wasn't my first choice."

"I bet you'll like it in no time. And with me as a partner, how could you not?"

Dani looks between the two of us. Her face scrunches and she bites her lip. I hope she doesn't think I like him. That's the last thing I need to deal with right now. But I don't tell Nick that I plan on dropping auto shop. He looks completely serious about being partners, and for some reason I can't bring myself to crush his hopes.

* * *

"How was school?" my mom asks the minute I walk in.

I drop my backpack by the coat closet. I glance up to find her standing in the doorway to the kitchen with her hands clasped in front of her and a forced hopeful look on her face.

"It was fine," I tell her, kicking off my shoes.

She looks at me expectantly. Guess *fine* is not going to be a good enough answer. "I got stuck in auto shop. I'm hoping to get out of it though."

She slumps against the door frame, dropping her clasped hands. "They put you in auto shop? Are you going to talk with your guidance counselor?"

I nod. "Yeah, I signed up for an appointment with one. It'll be a bit before they can squeeze me in."

This is the first normal conversation we've had in almost a

year. And it's weird to have this back and forth. Almost like things are starting to settle.

"It could be fun," she says trying to perk up. "Being with all those boys. I bet there's at least one cute one to catch your eye."

And just like that, I shut down. There will be no cute boys catching my eye. I head for the stairs.

"I'm going to head up to my room," I say without bothering to look back. She probably looks disappointed that I'm ending this conversation. But it was taking a turn that I've got no desire to go down.

I haul myself up the stairs to my room and take refuge in my bed.

I plug in my headphones and collapse on top of the blankets. The singer, Birdy, flows into my ears, her voice soothing the tension in my body, allowing it to relax. I have no clue what to do about auto shop, but it's got to change. The looks Mr. Jack gave me, you'd think I was a frightened rabbit. I might want to run from the class screaming, but I won't.

My phone buzzes with a text. Whose number is this?

Unknown: Hey. Hope this is cool. Dani gave me your #

Who the hell did she give my number to?

Me: Who is this?

Unknown: Nick

Crap. I put my phone down with shaky hands. What's his plan? Guys just don't start texting girls unless they want something. They always want something.

My phone buzzes again.

Nick: Should Dani not have given me your #?

Too late for that now.

Me: No, it's fine

Nick: Good

I wait for more, but thankfully that's it. I can't believe she gave him my number. Great. She'll probably ask me a million questions later. I've got no interest in him, and frankly I don't even know if I could be friends with him. But for some reason I find myself adding his number into my phone anyway.

* * *

"She emerges from her cave." My dad's dramatic voice carries from the kitchen as I hit the bottom of the stairs.

"Very funny."

He taps a hand on the kitchen table. "Hey, Sweets. Come have a seat and tell me about your first day."

My mom stands at the stove, trying to appear like she's completely engrossed in whatever she's cooking, but we all know that isn't the case. I take a seat next to my dad, dreading the interrogation.

"Mom says you're in auto shop?"

He looks as confused as I feel. I fill him in on what I'm sure he already heard from Mom. "Now I'm stuck working on some project where my partner is rebuilding an engine."

Dad bites his lip like he's trying really hard not to laugh. "You can laugh now, but you better not laugh when I fail," I tell him in all seriousness.

"You'll do fine. You always bounce back."

Everyone freezes at a phrase he always used to say to me. I haven't heard it in almost a year. Anytime something didn't go my way, he would tell me that it was okay because I always bounce back. But right now we all know that isn't happening. Most days I don't want it to happen. And there are a few moments where I wish I could go back to the life I had, but dark memories immediately cloud my brain, shutting out any light.

The atmosphere in the room plummets. And where we used to have laughter-filled meals, it's now tense and stilted. The constant worried looks between my parents don't help, either. Dad clears his throat. "Don't worry, Sweets. You'll tackle that class."

Will I? Maybe the past Tori would have. I know my dad is hoping to see the person I used to be, but I'm not even sure who I am now. And I don't know how to change that.

6

I wipe the grit away from my eyes. I didn't sleep at all last night. Anytime my eyes closed, visions of last year held me in a terror-filled grip. I got dressed for school way before I even heard my dad stir and leave for work.

Now I'm hiding out in my room, waiting until Dani texts. One look at me and Mom will know something is up.

My phone buzzes and her name pops up. I make my way quietly down the stairs. I glance out the front window as Dani's car pulls into the driveway. I look at the passenger seat, thankfully no one's in it.

"Bye, mom!" I yell as I run out the door before she can give me any encouraging remarks or bring up cute boys.

I drop into the car and turn to Dani. "Hey."

She lets out an annoyed huff. Great way to start the day.

"Something wrong?" I ask.

She backs out of the driveway without acknowledging my question. I can wait her out.

"Nick text you?" she finally asks.

Ahh, so that's why she's mad. "Yeah, last night. Why did you give him my number?"

"He asked," she says like it didn't bug her to do it.

"You know I don't like him, right? I have no interest in him in *that* way. We have to do a project together."

She shrugs and doesn't take her eyes off the road. "Why would it matter to me?" she asks.

Guess we're pretending that she doesn't like him. All right. "I just wanted you to know, that's all."

"Okay," she says. She must be good with my response, because soon she goes into some gossip involving a gym teacher. But I tune her out, happy to avert one crisis.

* * *

I walk into homeroom with Regina and we take our seats. Nick comes in the door and heads straight for us. His eyes get super bright and a smile stretches across his face as soon as he sees me. Regina's face pinches as she looks at where is gaze is directed. How do I tell her it's nothing? How do I tell her not to freak out and tell Dani about this?

As Nick makes his way closer, the phone on Mr. Knell's desk rings and he picks it up. His gaze immediately hones in on me. He hangs up, but his eyes don't leave me.

"Victoria, Mrs. Martha in the guidance counseling office wants to see you," Mr. Knell tells me.

Yes! I thought I had to wait until next week, but hallelujah. If it wouldn't look so weird, I'd totally do a fist-pump in the air right now. I grab my bag and rush out of my seat before Nick gets to me. He waves at me as I leave out the door, but I don't acknowledge it. Maybe he'll stop trying.

I walk toward the principal's office, assuming that I'll hit the guidance counselor's office on the way. Thankfully Mrs. Martha's office is right next to the main one, so I walk in without knocking.

Is that—?

Yup, that's a life-size Gene Simmons KISS doll. I've unfortunately had to see too many photos of him from when my dad went to their concerts back in the day.

I look back at the door and double check the name on it. This really *is* the counselor's office. Where is she? I scan the room, taking in the concert posters. Apparently, she's a huge—huge being an understatement—fan of 80s hair bands.

"Hey there!"

A body pops up from beneath the desk, and I'm pretty sure my heart just stopped. I grab the chair in front of me so I don't crumple to my knees. She looks at my expectantly, and I'm sure my face is still stuck in a bug-eyed position. Does she not realize I'm struggling to breathe here? Who hides behind a desk and pops up like a freaking whack-a-mole?

"Victoria?" the crazy 80s-lover asks. "Are you okay, sweetie?"

I grip my shirt above my chest. "I think I just had a mini heart attack."

She blinks at me from behind black-rimmed glasses. "Sorry. What was that?"

I wave her off. "Never mind."

She tilts her head like a bird, looking at me like I'm the crazy one. "Why don't you have a seat?"

"Sure, just let me release the death grip I have on the chair," I mutter.

She opens a file on her desk and then graces me with an overly large smile. "Welcome to Saybrooke High School. Bet it's a lot different than Arizona. Oh, I'm Mrs. Martha, by the way."

I nod because this is like the twentieth time I've heard *that* comment about Arizona.

She squints at me, scrutinizing something but I'm not sure

what. She nods, apparently coming to some sort of conclusion. "Not a big talker, but that's okay. What brings you to see me today?"

I sit up in my seat. "I was wondering if you could switch me out of auto class."

She turns toward her computer. "Let me just pull up what's available."

She hums what I think is a Def Leopard song as she plucks away at the computer keys. I rub at my cuffs, silently begging whatever higher power there is that something else is open.

She taps a few more keys until a frown mars her face. "Hmm, I'm not seeing anything. Don't you like being with all those boys?"

"No." One word, but there's so much emotion in it that she looks up from her computer and stares straight into my eyes.

"Do you want to tell me why?"

I break my stare, focusing on the creepy KISS doll hanging out behind her. "Not really."

"Victoria, look at me, please." Her request is soft, so I fight the need to hide and look instead toward her.

"There's nothing else available right now, and you *need* this class. Obviously, auto shop makes you uncomfortable," she hesitates, "but they're not all *bad* guys."

It's the way she looks at me when she says the word *bad* that makes the color drain from my face. Does she know? *No one* knows. She can't know.

She reaches into her purse. "I'm not going to pry, but I want you to take this card and give the number a call. Her name is Dr. Marie West. She's a therapist, and really helped me when I needed it."

I take the card and shove it into my jeans pocket. Mrs. Martha takes off her glasses and cleans them on her shirt while she holds my gaze. "You don't have to live with this burden alone. Let someone share it."

My throat tightens and I drop my gaze to try to get myself together. This lady just met me, and she already knows things about me that no one else does. She understands something that most people don't. And it feels like we're part of an awful club, one that no one wants to be a member of.

She puts her glasses back on and leans forward. "I'll make you a deal. Because there's nothing else available, I'll stop in when you have that class. That way you'll have a little extra estrogen in there and maybe it'll help."

I manage to choke out, "Okay."

"Good," she says, forcing cheer into her voice. "Now remember to call that number, and I'll see you in fifth period. Oh, and just think of Mr. Jack as Santa. Makes him a lot less intimidating. Trust me, it'll help."

I rise from the chair and basically flee the room, heading for the bathroom. I duck into a stall and sit down. I need to get my crap together.

I pull the card out of my pocket. Dr. Marie West. This lady can't help me; none of the others could. In the past eight months I've been forced to sit down with a number of therapists that have either tried to be my friend to get me talking or asked me endless questions that I don't want to answer. I'm about to tear the card in two, but the bathroom door bangs open and I jam it back into my jeans.

"Did you see the new girl?" a girl asks.

I hang my head. Seriously? They had to come into the bathroom at this moment? Now I'm stuck in here.

"Yeah, she's pretty. She'd be even more if she wore different clothes," another, with an oddly deep voice, responds.

"Definitely," the first adds.

This is not the conversation I thought would happen. This totally felt like the beginnings of a *Hallmark* movie my mom watched the other day. Except some girl was trapped in the guys' bathroom. But I'm really surprised there isn't the usual bashing. Or maybe that's just a television thing? Or maybe I'm that jaded.

Apparently I'm not that big of a subject, because they start talking about some cute guy. But I can't leave the stall now because how weird would that be? Shoot, I wonder if they can see my feet. They probably think there's a girl sitting here spying on them or having bathroom issues. They really need to get on with it and leave.

"Did you see Nick today?" the first girl asks, and I stop counting ceiling tiles. Are they talking about the Nick I know?

"Nick Janus?" I perk up at the name. Oh, that's definitely him. "Yeah, he looks so lickable today." Her voice takes on a serious raspy tone as she talks about him.

Wait, did she just describe Nick as...lickable? I bite down on my lower lip to hold back my hysterical laughter. I don't know if I'll be able to look at him again without thinking about these girls' comments. I have to tell Dani.

The bell rings, unfortunately cutting off their conversation about Nick. They scram out of the bathroom and I finally escape from the stall. My reflection in the mirror catches me by surprise. When's the last time a genuine smile graced my face? My eyes catch on my cuffs and the smile instantly drops.

The warning bell rings, and I head toward class.

* * *

"You are not going to believe what I overheard today," I tell Dani as I sit down next to her with my lunch.

Her eyes roam my face. "It must be something good for you to crack a smile."

I ignore her comment, because sadly it's true. "So, I was in the girl's bathroom and two girls came in. They started talking about Nick and one said he was *lickable*. I'm not sure that's even a word."

Dani's eyes go wide and she snorts. "Stop it, you aren't serious."

"No, really, but it was kind of weird because the one that called him that, her voice went like super husky when she started talking about him. Guessing there's a bunch of girls crushing on him."

"Oh, this is great! I so have to tease him about that later."

"I thought you'd appreciate that little bit of gossip. But seriously, of all the things to describe him as, they went with lickable?"

Dani pats my shoulder like I'm a poor, naïve child. "We need you to get out more so you can find out your own definition of guys that are lickable."

I tense; I don't want any *dating* help from Dani. "Can we stop saying lickable? Because—"

"Who's lickable?" a voice interrupts me.

Ugh, enough with that freaking word already.

I turn to see Nick's smiling face. Well, this just got a ton more awkward. Thankfully Dani leans forward, more than happy to fill him in on what I heard, so I don't have to tell him. I get the feeling the more we interact, the more he's going to get the impression I want to be friends. And I just *can't* handle that right now.

7

―――――

"You really heard girls calling me that?" Nick asks as we sit at our table in auto shop.

"You need to stop eavesdropping on conversations," I tell him. "And if I hear that word one more time I'm going to scream."

He leans over the table, typing into his phone. "Are you telling me that if a bunch of guys said that about you, you wouldn't be interested?"

A cold chill works its way down my body. "No, I wouldn't."

He moves his eyes away from his phone to my face at the change in my tone. I'm dead serious with him right now. I hope I never hear that coming out of some guy's mouth. "Yeah, it probably would be a little weird coming from a bunch of guys."

"Good afternoon, gentlemen, oh, sorry—and lady," Mr. Jack says, his voice landing like a bomb within the auto shop.

I sink lower in my seat a little bit as the class full of guys stares at me. I really want to tell them to quit staring, since I was here yesterday, but I keep my eyes forward.

"Today you'll be working on your project," he continues.

Wonderful.

"I want you ready to present your ideas next week to the class. Go ahead and get with your partner."

Nick slides his chair closer to mine. Has he never heard of personal space? I scoot a little away and he thankfully ignores that. He opens his notebook and we get straight to business. Thank goodness.

"Zack and I've been working on a 1969 Chevy Camaro," he says like I should either know what that is or be impressed. News flash: I am neither.

I stare at him with a blank face.

"Do you know what that is?" he asks.

"Besides the fact that it's a car? I believe I told you yesterday that all I know is how to put gas in a car. And I can also tell the difference between a minivan and an SUV, but that's about the extent of it."

"So then, your answer is no?" he asks.

"Correct."

He shakes his head, his face contorted in mock horror. "All right, let me pull up a photo," he says. He gets his phone out and pulls up a picture. The car is black, sleek, and looks like it's meant for speed.

"Nice," I tell him. I mean I like that color, but I'm not sure what else to say.

"She's a beauty," he says, still looking at the picture.

"She?" I ask.

"Yeah, all cars are girls." He says this like it's a known fact. Interesting.

"Our girl doesn't look like this yet, but she will." Did he just lovingly stroke the photo, or did I imagine that?

"Should I leave you two alone?" I ask.

He finally glances up, laughing. "Sorry. I just love cars."

"I kinda got that."

He puts his phone away. "Anyways, Zack and I always planned

on redoing the engine for this project. Guess you'll be doing this with me."

This is so important to him, and that really makes me nervous. "I doubt I'll be much help," I tell him, because it's true and I don't want to ruin this. This is important to him, and while I'd rather not fail a class, I could skate by with a C and be happy.

"Don't worry, I'll show you what to do. It won't be that bad." He delves into all the different parts that he already has and the ones he's missing. I try to stay focused, but he lost me at the word *solenoid*.

"Sound good?" he asks as the bell rings.

"Sure," I respond, sounding unsure even to myself.

He lifts a brow.

"Just tell me what to do and we'll get it done," I tell him. At least I hope we'll get it done.

8

AFTER SCHOOL I WALK IN THE FRONT DOOR, IMMEDIATELY SPOTTING my dad on the couch. "What are you doing home from work so early?" I ask as I take off my coat and shoes. Nothing good ever happens when he comes home early.

He leans forward and clasps his hands between his knees. "We need to talk," he says in a gruff voice.

I freeze and take a deep breath. Really, doesn't he know that's like the worst phrase in the English language to say to someone? Nothing good ever happens after you hear "We need to talk." What they really should say is, "Hey, I'm about to drop some bad news on you, so be prepared."

"Okay..." I draw out the word.

He takes a deep breath and then sets his face into a determined stare: straight mouth, thin lips, and a little squinting of the eye. His serious dad face.

"Now, your mom doesn't want to push, but I will because I think you need it. You need to pick a new therapist and make an appointment. Remember our agreement?"

Shame floods me. Like I could forget. When he picked me up

from the Valleywise Behavioral Health Center, with tears in his eyes, he made me promise to be in therapy. In return he promised to give me whatever space I needed, and not to push about what happened. As long as I kept seeing a therapist.

I grab my bag and dig into the front pocket, remembering the card Mrs. Martha gave me. "I think I found one," I tell him, handing it over.

He looks the card over. "It has to a be a real therapist, not some new-age quack."

"I doubt she is, my guidance counselor gave me the card."

"Oh. Okay, well, good. That's good." He gets up from the couch and hands the card back to me, giving my hand a little squeeze. "Let me know when your appointment is, and I'll take you."

"Sure," I tell him, looking at his hand around mine.

He squeezes it again and I look up. "I love you, kid. The only reason I'm pushing you is because I know you're still hurting."

He leans down and kisses the top of my head and walks out of the room. It's good that he doesn't look back, because I don't think either of us can handle watching the tears streaming down my cheeks. Sometimes I think it's more painful that he knows I'm hurting versus the hurt I feel.

* * *

At least this therapist's office looks normal. All the others I've seen tried to have a *cool* office. Some had beanbag chairs—one even had a freaking lava lamp—but my *favorite* was the one with the blow-up clown. Forget the fact that clowns are creepy in general, but a blow-up one you're supposed to punch? Only lasted five minutes in that office.

But this place looks like she's not trying too hard. The reception area is pretty basic, with couches and some green plants that are thriving, which hopefully bodes well for this therapist. Out of everything, the art is awesome. The bold colors and jagged lines are amazing. It kind of looks like maybe one of her patients painted them. It's *that* kind of crazy.

"Victoria?"

Dr. Marie West stands in her doorway. She's probably in her late forties, or at least old enough to be my mom. She's totally polished though, with her blunt blonde bob, evergreen sweater, and black dress pants. Her eyes are kind though. Not like the other therapists who either looked disinterested or way too eager.

I stand up and Dr. West gives me a small, friendly smile.

"Come on in," she says, and walks back into her office.

I follow her in and sit in one of the huge leather chairs bracketing her desk. Hanging on the wall behind her are her degrees and certificates. *Well, at least she seems legit.*

"No couch?" I ask, looking around.

"It's behind you." Her voice is very matter of fact, like she's picking up on my stall tactics.

"So it is" is apparently my witty reply.

She leans back in her chair. "Did you want to lie on the couch?" She seems generally interested to know.

"Nope, I'm good right here." I give the chair a pat like it's a dog or something. *Geez.*

We stare at one another for several long beats of silence.

She sits forward and places her hands flat on her desk. "You contacted me, Victoria; why is that?"

All right, we're getting right to the point. No weird get-to-know-you games for this lady. But that's kind of nice. "My school counselor gave me your card. And my parents said I had to start seeing a new therapist since we moved here."

She opens a folder on her desk. "Yes, I see you moved here from Arizona."

I wonder if that folder has notes from previous doctors saying that trying to get me to talk is a waste of time. I bet it says something like "patient is difficult."

She keeps reading from it. "Your file talks a lot about your panic attacks." She looks up and catches my eye. "Are you still having them?"

What *doesn't* it say in there? "Yup." No point in lying.

"How do you cope with them?" She appears genuinely curious. That's a first. Usually, I get lectured with a long list of ways to cope, but rarely did they seem like they wanted to know which ones worked.

Does shutting myself in a closet for hours on end count as coping? "I just...do?"

Her eyes lock with mine, and I don't like the feeling of her reading me. It's like she's pulling back the layers and seeing behind all the crap I'm spewing at her. "Well, I'm glad you have some way in which you cope. But would it be okay if I give you one technique and you can see if it works the next time you feel a panic attack coming on?"

"Sure," I say in a nonchalant manner, but on the inside, I'm begging on my knees for a way to deal.

She relaxes into her seat and I do the same without meaning to. "When you feel like everything is crashing down around you, I want you to try breathing in slowly, while counting to ten. Hold that breath for ten. Then, exhale slowly and count down from ten. It'll take a couple of rounds of counting to get your breath to slow, but it will."

"That's it?" Why does this seem like something I could've Googled?

"Yes. For some it works, some it doesn't. It may sound too easy, but try it and see if it helps."

"Okay," I say, my voice heavy with uncertainty. It can't be that easy.

We sit in silence, staring at one another. Shouldn't she be

bombarding me with questions? I fidget in my seat, not really knowing what to do with my hands.

"I'm never going to push you to talk," she finally says. "That's not what I'm here for. When you feel like it, we will."

* * *

"How was it?" my dad asks as I climb in the car.

I look over at him as he puts the car in reverse. "Fine." That feels like a safe answer.

He opens his mouth and then closes it again. I wait. This waiting game has become the norm over the last several months. He chooses his words carefully with me now.

"You know you can talk to me, Tori," he says, eyes on the road.

I lean my head against the window and stare at the slushy, brown snow lining the roads. I doubt he really means it. What dad wants to hear about the dark secrets his teenage daughter is hiding? Especially the ones that drove her to attempt suicide?

"Okay," I answer for his benefit.

"I'm serious, Tori."

I look over at him. His face is set in a hard line. His serious face.

"I know your mom can be"—he tilts his head back and forth—"a little watchful."

That's putting it lightly. She's a hovering mess.

"But I'm not going to baby you. I just want you to know I'm here."

It's hard to take him seriously. After I left the hospital it was like he couldn't talk to me. He hardly stayed in the same room with me. Every time he saw me his eyes would tear up and he would leave the room. I think I broke his heart. How does he expect me to tell him things now?

"And give your mom some time. She'll calm back down."

I broke this family. My mom is messed up because of me and my dad's walking on eggshells—it might be too little too late because there's no going back to how things once were. We're not that family anymore. How come I can see that, and he can't?

I let out a deep sigh. "Sure, Dad."

His knuckles are white against the steering wheel. He doesn't believe my words any more than I believe his.

9
—————

A week later, and even though Nick's been telling me all about cars and engines any chance he gets, I'm still at a loss. The only positive thing? I'm not having panic attacks from auto shop anymore. Oh, I'm not really liking the class and I still haven't been able to picture Mr. Jack as Santa, but it's getting better. And I haven't been able to say that about anything in a long time. But I'm dreading standing in front of class today and sharing the plans for our project.

"Nick and Tori, you're up next," Mr. Jack announces.

Nick leans close to me, close enough that I smell a faint whiff of his Old Spice deodorant, and it makes my body lock tight at the memory of someone else who smelled the same. My heart races, and my wrists start to burn.

"Don't worry." Nick's voice drags me away from a memory I don't want to relive. "I'll do most of the talking. You just stand there and try not to scowl so much."

What? I whip my head toward him. "I don't scowl."

He points to my face. "You are right now," he says.

48

I touch my face. Damn it, he's right. "Well, it's because you piss me off."

He laughs and stands from his seat. I follow him up to the front with my arms crossed tightly across my chest.

"Tori and I are working on rebuilding an engine for a 1969 Chevy Camaro," Nick tells the class full of guys. This gets a lot of shouts from the room. Guess it's a popular car.

Nick goes on to explain the different parts that need to be swapped out, along with all the cleaning and degreasing we have to do. I just stand there, apparently trying not to scowl.

"Now Tori, what are you planning on contributing to this project?" Mr. Jack asks from his seat at his desk.

Before I can even open my mouth, some jerk from the back pipes in. "She's going to be the hood ornament."

This gets laughs and high fives from various guys in class. I freeze and I can feel the blood drain from my face. Mr. Jack unfolds to his full height and the class goes deadly quiet when they see his thunderous expression. "Shut it, Rossi, or I'm docking your grade. I won't tolerate that in my classroom." His eyes touch on the rest of the guys in the room, silently letting them know that this applies to them too.

He looks back toward me for my answer to his original question, but all I see are guys leering at me, fantasizing how I'd look laid out on a hood of a car.

My palms tremble, and my chest is being squeezed by a vice. When did it get so hot in here? He's waiting for an answer, but I can't even open my mouth to speak. I frantically search the room for the door. There. I could make a break for it before anyone could catch me. A flash of brown snags my attention. I squint my eyes. What is that?

Mrs. Martha stands at the window on the door, her hair teased out to extreme measures. She waves at me and then breezes into the room. "What am I missing?" she asks.

"Oh, hello, Mrs. Martha," Mr. Jack says. "Tori was just about to talk to us about her project with Nick."

She settles into a seat right in front of me and locks her eyes with mine. "How interesting. Go ahead, Tori. I know nothing about cars, but I'm sure it'll be fascinating."

I keep my eyes only on her and try counting to ten while I take a deep breath like Dr. West told me. I let it out slowly, counting down from ten. Before I reach six, everyone else fades and I know I can talk. "I'll probably just do whatever Nick tells me. It can't be too hard to clean car parts. I don't know much about cars."

"Well, that sounds good, doesn't it, Mr. Jack?" Mrs. Martha asks.

"Yes, it does," he says, clapping his hands. "This sounds promising, guys—oh, and gal. One of these days I'll get that right. Let's see who is up next."

Nick and I return to our seats. "Hey Nick, she said she'd do whatever you ask. I'd take advantage of that," I hear Rossi's low voice behind us.

My spine snaps straight and a cold chill slides down my back.

"Don't be a dick, Rossi," Nick replies.

"Yeah, not cool man," I hear the guy next to Rossi mutter.

I want to thank Nick, but more than anything I need this class to be over so I can get the hell out of here. So like usual, I pretend it didn't happen.

* * *

"How was auto today?" Dani asks when I join her at the lunch table.

"Some guy named Rossi is a jerk," I tell her, slamming my lunch down.

She nods her head in understanding. Apparently, I'm not the

only one who thinks this. "He suggested Tori be a hood ornament," Nick adds, barely leashing the anger in his voice.

Dani looks between the two of us, picking up on the thick tension. "What?" she asks.

"He wants me lying naked on the hood of the car," I tell her, my voice lacking any amusement.

Dani gasps and Nick lets out a muttered curse.

"You know," Dani says with a thoughtful look on her face. "Under all those baggy clothes, you do have the body for it."

Nick chokes on his slice of pizza.

"Never going to happen," I tell them.

"I mean..." Nick mutters.

Everyone at the table freezes and Dani kicks him in the shin. "What the hell?" he yells.

"Don't be a pig," she says, glaring at him.

"I was just kidding, geez," he says rubbing his leg. "Just trying to lighten the mood."

"Thanks," I tell her, ignoring Nick. And I mean it. This conversation needs to be over with.

"Anytime," Dani says. "Oh, hey, my mom and I are coming over for dinner tonight."

Awesome. And there's the nail in the coffin for my day— having to deal with Dani's mom.

10

"How are you adjusting to living here, Tori?" Kris asks as she spoons some rice onto her plate.

I hate the way she watches me with those shrewd gray eyes. I don't know what she's looking for, but it's freaking annoying.

"Fine," I answer, smoothing the napkin on my lap.

She makes a humming noise like she doesn't believe me. Does she know something that I don't? I grab my cup and take a drink. "I heard you found a new therapist," she says.

I slam my cup down onto the table and shoot a glare at my mother, who just averts her eyes. Nice. This isn't my mom. I don't know who this woman is, but this isn't the mother I grew up with anymore. *My mom* wouldn't stand for any of this crap. I spear Kris with a pissed-off look. "Not that it's any of your business, but yes, I have."

Kris gasps. "There's no need for that tone," she says.

Dani stares down at the chicken she's currently picking to the death on her plate, while the rest of the table pauses at the heavy tension pressing down on us. Who the hell does Kris think she is? And why is my mom telling her all this stuff about me? My life is none of her business. She's got no clue. "You're not my mom, so stay the hell out of it."

"Tori," my mom tries to reprimand me.

"Well—" Kris starts, but my dad finally wades in.

"Enough. We're supposed to be having dinner. Thanks for your concern, Kris, but this is a family issue." He says the last part while looking at my mom.

"I've lost my appetite," I say and grab my plate, not waiting for either of my parents' reactions.

"Me too," Dani adds, rising from the table with me.

I dump my dinner in the trash and head out of the kitchen with Dani in tow. We make our way upstairs and to my room.

"Sorry about my mom," she says while she lowers herself to the floor in front of my desk chair.

I join her on the ground and lean against my bed. "It's embarrassing," I tell her, my eyes trained to the ceiling. And it is. It's bad enough that they know I tried committing suicide. I have no desire to discuss it with Kris, Dani, or my parents, ever. We slide into an uneasy silence. Does Kris think she's helping by wading into my business? I just don't get that woman. Dani's so different from her mom. Well, she does love gossip like Kris, but she never pushes people like her mom does.

My phone chimes with a text and I look down at it.

Nick: Come watch me play basketball tomorrow?

"Who's that?" Dani asks, leaning over to see my cell.

"Nick," I tell her, lifting up my phone.

"Do you guys text all the time?" she asks, sounding suspicious.

"No, he was just saying that he's playing tomorrow."

Her body relaxes back against my desk chair. "Oh yeah, boys' basketball is tomorrow night." She doesn't sound completely convinced, but the last thing I want is to tell her that Nick wants me to come watch him. It's not really lying, but it'll give her the wrong impression about him and me. But the idea of dating or hanging out with any guys right now makes me sick to my stomach.

"You should come with us and watch him play," she says.

"Maybe," I tell her, not sure if she actually wants me to go. Or if I want to go either.

"Dani, let's go," Kris calls from downstairs.

She gets up to leave. "Let me know tomorrow if you want to come."

"I will."

She walks out of my room and I wait for the sound of the front door opening and then closing before I pick up my phone. I stare at the screen, trying to think of just what to say.

Me: Maybe

"Are you going to go?" my mom asks from the doorway, causing me to drop my phone. She takes a step like she's going to walk into my room, but stops herself mid-step.

"Go where?" I ask.

"I think it would be good if you went to the basketball game." Guess she was listening to my conversation with Dani. While it ticks me off, I'm not really surprised. "Get out of the house, Tori, and have some fun. Maybe while you're out, your dad and I will go grab dinner."

I drop my head back against my bed. "You guys don't need me to be out of the house just so you can have a date."

"We can't leave you home alone," she says in a strained whisper.

I lift my head and look at her face. Is this what we've come to? Does she really not trust me to be by myself? Do I need to be babysat now? "Mom, nothing is going to happen," I say carefully.

Her eyes drift to my wrists lying in my lap. They're covered, but I know what she sees. She sees me on the bathroom floor, bleeding from where I cut them.

"I can't count on that, baby. Tell Dani you'll go with her tomorrow."

She walks out of the room, completely ignoring any of my protests. I chuck the phone across the room and it bounces off the door. I can make my own decisions.

And I didn't even get to grill her about spreading our business to Kris.

* * *

I pull open the gym door and frown at Dani. "How on earth did I let you talk me into this?"

Dani stops looking at her phone and her lips spread into a huge cheesy smile. "Because you *love* me."

"Yeah, I don't think that's it."

She shrugs and goes back to her phone. "Well, it helped that your mom heard me when I asked."

Ahh, yes. My mother talked for hours after school about me going out so she and my dad could have some "alone time." It was hard to fight her on it when she looked so excited. There was also the fact that Nick had asked me if I was going, but that had no sway in me being here. "Promise not to ditch me," I beg her.

She looks up from her phone again. "Why would I ditch you?"

I point at her phone. "Who's texting you right now?"

Her cheeks flame and I lift a brow. "Promise not to ditch me with whoever you're texting right now," I insist.

"Fine, I won't, but it's just Nick," she says, avoiding looking at my face.

"How long have you liked him?"

Her eyes get huge and she looks around like she's afraid someone just heard us. "Tori, shut up," she says, her words are sharp like a whip. "It's not like that, we're just friends."

"Sure..." Guess we're telling fairy tales today.

We climb the bleachers to the rest of her friends. "Hey guys!" she yells.

Everyone turns and spots us. And thus ensues the many hugs like we just didn't see each other three hours ago at school. Thank goodness no one squeals; I think I'd have to leave on principle if they did.

"I don't know if you've all met her yet, but this is my friend Tori," Dani says to a group of people I've seen in the halls at school but haven't had any classes or lunch with.

I give a small wave and get a lot of "heys" in response. I turn toward the court as our team rushes out of the locker room.

"Doug, scoot down so we can squeeze in," Dani says, looking past my shoulder.

I turn back and see a lanky guy sitting on the bench. His eyes survey my face and I wish I had worn my beanie tonight. He shifts so that we have to sit in between him and Regina. I move quickly to sit next to her. Thankfully Dani is too engrossed in her phone to notice.

"Hey, your friend's kind of cute," I hear Doug whisper to Dani.

My eyes stay trained on the basketball court, but I don't really see it. I start to take deep breaths as my stomach starts to twist.

"I know, right? She's a total knockout when she's got girly clothes on," Dani tells him, trying to be quiet, but we can all hear her.

What the hell is wrong with her? She needs to stop talking right now. "Really?" he asks, and there's that tone that I hate. Such a simple question coming from his lips, but I swear I can almost feel his greedy eyes roving from my legs, up to my hips, over my breasts, and then my face.

They need to stop. My hands start to fist, and my feet begin to tap. Dani's phone dings and I almost drop to my knees in a prayer of thanks.

I look for a distraction other than our team getting ready for the tip off. "Hey, Regina, are we any good?" I ask, silently hoping she doesn't hear my voice shake.

She stops the conversation she's having with the girl next to her and turns to me. "Oh, yeah, we won state last year. I don't know how it will go without Zack, but they should be able to pull it off."

"This Zack guy was like a legend around here, huh?"

"Yeah, pretty much. I wish you could have met him—you would have loved him."

I highly doubt that, but I'm not about to burst her bubble. Out of the corner of my eye I see Nick steal the ball from the opposing team. "Hey look, Nick's got the ball," I tell her.

Dani springs from her and seat and starts jumping up and down screaming Nick's name next to me. I crack a smile. "Did I just see *you* smile?" Regina asks.

"It does happen on occasion," I tell her, keeping my eyes on the game. I smile, it's just I haven't found anything to smile at in a while.

I watch Nick on the court, he's pretty amazing out there. I had no clue.

He lines up at the 3-point line and launches the ball toward the basket. Nothing but net. "Wow," I whisper to myself.

"You should have seen him play with Zack. Those two worked the court like you wouldn't believe," Doug says, leaning behind Dani so he can talk to me directly. I glance over, expecting his face would be all leering eyes, but they're not. He's got a friendly face and nothing else.

"That's cool," I tell him, turning back toward the court.

"You just moved here, right?" he asks.

"Yup." I keep my eyes on the game.

"From Arizona?"

"Yup."

He lets out a small laugh and I finally look over at him. He's grinning. "Do you have a quota on word usage or something?"

His quip totally takes me off guard and I laugh—a real genuine one.

Everyone around us freezes. You would think I just threatened to blow up the school or something. "What?" I ask, looking around.

"You smiled a minute ago, and now you laughed," Gretchen says from down the row. "Did you guys start drinking before you came?"

My face pulls into a frown.

"Now there's the Tori we know," Dani says pointing at my face.

"Do I never laugh?" I ask. It's an honest question, but a sad one.

"That's the first time I've heard you ," Regina says.

I didn't use to be like this. I used to laugh all the time, and it was rare that anyone saw me without a smile. But I can't tell them that there's not much for me to laugh or smile at anymore. Instead, I stick with my foolproof sarcasm. "You should have recorded that for posterity's sake then."

Doug laughs, while Regina looks slightly confused.

The crowd erupts again, snagging my attention back to the court. We're up by fifteen points. I guess we *are* pretty good. Nick runs back down the court, slapping the hands of his teammates. He stops at the top of the key, waiting and watching as the player with the ball moves toward him. In a flash, Nick intercepts a pass and is sprinting down the court to the basket. The crowd cheers again as he makes a layup, scoring two more points for Saybrooke.

The cheer squad busts out tumbling tricks in front of us, and a small sense of longing washes over me. It's like watching what my life would have been if things hadn't happened. We wouldn't be here in Connecticut, but I'd be at my old high school, Westwood, flipping and cheering for our boys.

"I hear you have auto shop with Nick," Doug says, leaning around Dani again, interrupting the show in front of me, but I'm sort of glad.

"Yup," I answer.

"That's it, Tori, move over." Dani gets up and squeezes in between me and Regina, putting me right next Doug.

Our legs touch as he leans into me, and I can smell the cigarette smoke on him. I just need to take deep breaths. We're at a basketball game. I'm with a bunch of people; nothing is going to happen. *Deep breaths.* If I have a full-blown panic attack I don't know if I'll be able to show my face around school again. They don't need to know how really messed up I am.

Doug laughs, not picking up on my freak-out at all. "Enough with the 'yups.' I'm trying to have a conversation with you."

We chat on and off during the game. I try to stay mushed to Dani's side so my legs don't touch his. If he's noticed my body language, he hasn't shown it.

The final buzzer rings, signaling the end of the game. No surprise we won by thirty points, crushing Guilford High. Dani and Regina jump up, screaming their heads off. They're louder than the cheerleaders.

"We're going to wait for Nick, and then we'll all head out to Deep River," Dani tells the group after they finally stop screaming.

"Wait, what's Deep River and what are we doing there?" I ask.

"We're going to the tracks," Doug says like I should already know this.

Coming to the game was one thing, but going somewhere else at night, with a group of people? Yeah, this isn't going to fly. "You want to just drop me off at home?" I ask Dani, because this probably isn't the best idea.

"No way; you're coming with us," she tells me, and there's not much I can do to stop her since she's my ride.

11

So, the tracks are freaking railroad tracks. I don't know where I thought we'd be going, but this wasn't it. "Umm isn't anyone worried about a train coming and hitting us?" I ask the obvious question, looking up and down the tracks.

And not only am I worried that we're going to have to run for cover, but both sides of the tracks are dense woods. As soon as we left the parking lot and started walking, we were shrouded in darkness.

"No, this is for the Essex Steam Train. It doesn't run at night," Nick tells me from a few feet away.

It still feels like a dumb idea walking down train tracks at night.

In the woods.

With people I barely know.

"Besides," Doug whispers from behind me, "it's not the trains you need to worry about at night. It's the ghosts."

I shrink away from his close proximity. I should have made Dani take me home. This feels like it's turning out to be a really bad idea. At any minute my heart is going to burst out of my chest from how fast it's beating.

"Apparently there was a battle close by and a bunch of people were killed. They're supposed to be buried around here somewhere," Nick says, like it's no big deal that we could be walking on people's graves.

Fantastic, let's just piss off a bunch of ghosts. This sounds like it'll be an *epic* night. "So, what are we doing?"

"Tori, just relax and try to have a good time," Gretchen yells from up ahead.

"Nick, come up here for a sec," Dani calls out.

Nick gives me a small smile and jogs ahead, leaving me very much alone with Doug. And I hate it. I try walking faster, but he keeps pace with me. "What's nice about being out here is how easy you can see the stars," Doug says.

Wait, is that a line? Is he hitting on me? I can't deal with this right now. I tuck my shaking hands into my coat pockets. Even though its freezing, sweat drips down my back. And those damn breathing techniques are not working.

"I guess so," I mutter, trying to put a little bit more distance between us, but he speeds up too.

"You know, we should hang out some time, just the two of us," he says, but there's a hesitation in his voice.

"Yeah." I don't even know why I said that. I swear my brain and my mouth are not communicating correctly right now.

I start to walk faster. My foot catches on a track and my arms fly out to break my fall, but Doug reaches out and wraps his arms around me, catching me.

My mind screams at the feel of him holding me, but my body freezes. "You're beautiful," he whispers, leaning close.

No. No. No!!! Please stop, please! I try and move my lips, but I can't form the words. He's too close. I feel his breath on my neck.

And the overwhelming stench of cigarettes makes my stomach roll.

My body and mind finally come together, and I push him off. "Don't....don't touch me." My voice comes out weak and raw. And I hate it. A sharp pain forms behind my eyes. I stagger away from him, my legs barely holding me up.

I force myself to get to Dani, leaving Doug standing alone looking rejected. "Dani, I need to go right now. I think I'm going to be sick," I tell her, gasping for breath.

"Wait, what?" she asks, immediately stepping away from me like I might puke on her.

"Are you okay, Tori?" Nick yells from down the tracks, but my focus stays on Dani.

She's got to see that there's more going on with me then possible puking, because she turns back around and heads with me to her car. "I'll be back, guys. I'm just going to take Tori home," she yells.

Everyone calls out to us, but neither of us respond. Doug says my name as we pass by, but I don't look at him. I'm too busy trying to hold myself together.

We pull out of the parking lot, and I can feel Dani's eyes darting between me and the road. "What's going on?" she asks.

I shake my head, not even trying to respond. I pull my knees up to my chest and lean my head against the cold window.

"Tori."

I close my eyes tight and pray we'll get to my house before I break down in front of her. No one needs to see that. And that string keeping me together is one fiber away from being obliterated.

The house is empty for once, and I couldn't be more grateful. I run up the stairs to the bathroom. Without turning on the lights I rush toward the shower and turn the hot water on full blast. The odor of his cigarettes still lingers on my skin, and it saturates my hoodie.

I tear my clothes from my body and stand under the scorching water, letting it pummel me. I grab my body wash and scrub my skin until it's raw. Tears make their way down my cheeks, but they're masked by the cascading water. Flashes from last year—of *him*—bring forth tortured sobs.

I crash to my knees on the shower floor, letting the water batter my back.

I don't want to think about that time.

A raw, anguished sound comes from deep within.

"Please. Please take it away," I whisper into the darkness.

But it doesn't go away; it just dulls a little with the fading warmth of the water. And once the water grows cold, I turn off the faucet and fumble for my robe and wrap it around myself. I slog into my room and stop short right in front of the mirror I let mom convince me to put back in my room. The weak girl staring back at me makes me sick. Memories flash in my mind from a year ago and tonight, mixing and confusing me, until I'm back in his car last summer.

It didn't matter that I said no. It didn't matter that I said I wasn't ready. He was tired of waiting. That's all that ever mattered, what he wanted. He saw my body as his and he wouldn't accept anything less. He took and took until I couldn't look at myself in the mirror anymore. He took until anyone's touch now makes me cringe. And he took until I decided I would rather die than let him have me anymore.

The unbearable pain keeps building. My muscles feel too tight. My fists clench and unclench while angry tears drip down my face. I try taking deep breaths like Dr. West told me. But it doesn't help; nothing helps. The glass cup on my nightstand beckons me. I debate for a second, but then the rage washes over me again and I grab it. With a piercing, agonizing scream I hurl it at the mirror. The glass shatters, crashing toward the ground.

It's not enough.

It's never enough.

Books, pictures, my clock—all go crashing to the floor. I turn toward my closet and rip my clothes off the rod with the hangers still attached. I pound my fists on the inner closet walls. "Why didn't they just let me die?" I shout to an empty house.

I bring my fist down on the closet wall again, harder this time, but instead of putting a hole in it, it rattles.

What?

The noise is the reprieve from my destruction that I need. I hit it again, with less force, and hear something that sounds like a door rattling. I knock around the wall, through barely any light, looking for its source, when I finally find a hollow sound. My fingers scrape the wall until I find a seam. My heart kicks into a frenzy. There's got to be a secret door or something. I follow the seam until I find a little knob. Man, this thing is so small, like the size of a jeans button, no wonder I never saw it before.

I pull on the knob, but it sticks, so I grab it with both hands and tug. The door swings open; behind it is pitch black. I run back toward my bed, ignoring the broken glass glittering in the moonlight. I'll have to clean it up before my mom gets home. I grab my phone and turn the flashlight on.

I walk to the back of the closet and shine the light into the doorway. It's just a small entrance, but at the back there's a ladder attached to the wall. I hunch down and duck into the small space. The ladder must lead to the attic. I didn't even know this house had one. With my phone in one hand, I climb the ladder only a few rungs, when I encounter the ceiling. I turn my phone toward the ceiling, looking for the way in. To the left are hinges so I place my hand on the right side and push. The wooden door slowly opens with a loud groan. I push harder and it slams open to the floor above.

I step up one more rung, just so my head can stick up above the hole I'm in. I take my phone and shine the light around. My breath catches. What the hell? The room is full.

12

Paintings, pictures, and a few car posters line the wooden walls. I scan around with my phone's flashlight until I spot a light switch near the top of the ladder. I flip it on, scattering the cramped space with light from a single bulb dangling from the roof. Kicked-up dust floats around me, disturbing a place that looks like no one has been in months.

The floors creak and groan as I make my way around, but pay it no mind. My eyes zero in on the photos of people I now know. Dani smiles at Nick in one, and in another Doug has his arm around Regina. My eyes quickly skip away from that one. But what really snags my attention is the guy hugging Britney. How did the camera manage to catch that emotion in their eyes? You can tell they love each other.

Wait, that's got to be Zack. These are his things.

The drawings snag me next. There are tons of them. Most of them are people. Some I recognize and some I don't.

"Wow," I whisper into the stillness. He's so talented.

I make my way to the lone dusty desk in the corner. It's covered in papers, pencils, and charcoal. Sitting on the edge of the desk is a large black book covered in dust. I blow it off, scattering it into the room. I flip through it quickly. This has got to be like an art journal or something. I turn back to the beginning.

The first few drawings are of a dark and stormy sea. They're beautiful and terrifying at the same time. As I keep scanning the pages, each image becomes darker. The feeling of the whole book changes. The lines on the page are harsher. Words like *doubt, ugly,* and *corrupt* are written within the drawings. One in particular catches me off guard.

It's a sketch of a cracked mirror. Zack's reflection gazes out, meeting mine. My heart falters. The look on his face—man, do I know it so well. It's raw and it's hurting. It looks just like mine did a moment ago. Why did he draw himself like this? As broken?

None of this make sense. These drawings don't portray the Zack everyone describes.

I'm not sure how long I stare at the sketch, but a car door slams, jarring me from my thoughts. I put the portfolio back on the desk, vowing to come back up here.

I scramble down the stairs, back into the closet, and shut the secret door. Tomorrow; I'll come back tomorrow.

I walk back into my room, only to step on a piece of broken glass.

"Son of a—"

I forgot about the broken mirror. Blood pools under my foot. What am I going to tell my parents? I can't hide this from them. Mom's going to think I tried to kill myself again.

I sit down on the floor, needing to see how deep the glass went. This is going to hurt.

I go to pull it out when my bedroom door opens.

"We're home, Tori—" My mom's voice stops at the sight of me on the floor, hands covered in blood.

"Adam!" she screams.

My dad's footsteps pound up the stairs. "What's going on?" he yells.

My mom points at me and my dad's face goes white.

"It's not what you think." Oh my gosh, that sounds so cliché. "I broke my mirror and when I went to grab the broom I stepped on a piece. It cut my foot. I was just checking how deep it was when Mom came in." The words fly out, hoping I'll bring my mom back from the edge.

My dad squats down in front of me, ignoring the entire mess I made in my room, and lifts up my foot. "It doesn't look too bad. Let's get you into the bathroom and clean this up."

My mom rushes from the room, her muffled sobs feel like knife cuts to my heart.

I hobble behind my dad as we go into the bathroom. He points to the tub for me to sit down on the edge. "How did the mirror break?" he asks, getting the first aid kit from under the sink.

"Accident," I say, not looking at him.

"And whatever heavy object hit it, did it just fly by itself toward the glass?" he asks.

I shrug and he sighs before sitting down on the toilet seat lid and motioning for my foot.

I don't make any noise as he pulls out the glass, but my whole body flinches. "Is it going to happen again?" he asks as he cleans the cut.

I don't know what to tell him. We both know that it wasn't an accident, but I can't predict whether or not that anger will surface again. There is one thing that I want him to understand, though. "I didn't try to kill myself, Dad."

"Okay." I can't tell if he believes me, but I need him to.

He grabs my hand, making me lock eyes with him. "I want you to make another appointment with Dr. West. Soon," he says in all seriousness.

"All right, Dad."

His shoulders sag at my agreement and he goes back to doctoring my foot in silence.

* * *

"What made you come back?" Dr. West asks, leaning back in her chair.

I squirm in my seat a little. After our first visit I planned on never coming back, but that idea was shattered to hell just like my mirror.

Her face stays open and calm as she waits patiently for me to respond. I wonder if they taught her that skill in college. I don't think I could wait this long. I'd probably be asking the person a million questions—

"Victoria?"

I shake my head, dispersing my wayward thoughts, and focus back on her. "When I first came in here, it was because I had to get a new therapist since we moved here. Orders from my parents."

"And now?" she asks, writing something down in her notebook.

In my head I pictured this would go so much smoother. All I've got to do is just calmly tell her about the mirror and my dad's concerns. But the words spew out of my mouth without my control. "It's exhausting living this way," I blurt out.

Her pen stops moving, and she gives me her full attention. "And what way is that?"

I rub my hands down my jean-clad thighs. I'm pretty sure she can hear the pounding of my heart.

I take a deep breath. "The constant 'okay' face. I won't say smiling face, because I hardly smile. But the walking on eggshells around my parents. The weight of secrets. I feel like I'm trudging through mud every day. It sucks." I fight the urge to cry and scream all at the same time.

There's a slight weight lifted in finally saying those words, but the feeling is fleeting. Because I know the moment I leave this office, all those thoughts and feelings are going to slam back into me.

"I won't pretend that I don't know you tried to commit suicide."

Thank heavens for that.

"What it doesn't say in your file is why, or what event, triggered that."

"Do we have to talk about that?" I ask, fidgeting in my seat

"Well, no. Not if you don't want to."

My body starts to deflate into the chair.

"But—" And just like that, any relief I had is gone. "If you really are tired of living this way, then eventually you'll need to share what happened. I won't ever make you talk when you're not ready. And nothing leaves this office. I won't discuss our visits with your parents unless there's an emergency."

I don't know if I trust that. And while her words and face look sincere, past experiences has taught me to be wary with therapists.

"I'm just not ready to tell that part." Honestly, I don't know if I'll ever want to tell or be ready.

"Okay, then do you want to tell me what happened that finally drove you in here today?" She looks down at the notebook on her desk.

I drag in a deep breath. Here goes nothing. "I had a panic attack standing in the middle of train tracks," I push the words out.

Her eyes snap to mine. "Were you"—she pauses, likes she's gauging her next words—"waiting for a train?"

"No. It was the Essex Steam Train's tracks. They don't run at night."

She takes a deep breath and clasps her hands on the top of the desk.

"I don't think jumping in front of a train is really my style," I try and reassure her.

Her eyebrows raise, but she pushes on. "What were you doing there?"

"Hanging out with some people after the basketball game."

"And what happened to cause the panic attack?"

I tuck my sweaty palms under my knees. My body automatically starts to rock back and forth. I keep picturing Doug leaning in, but it's not Doug's face anymore—it's *his*. My breathing picks up and I'm losing feeling in my hands from the constant rocking. "This guy got too close to me and it felt like he might try to kiss me," I manage to say.

"I'm guessing you didn't want him to." It's not a question.

I shake my head. "I don't like being touched." At least not anymore. "I came home, and my parents were gone, and I just totally broke down. I kept picturing *him*. I broke my mirror and went crazy. Well...a little more crazy than usual."

"Did this guy try anything else?"

"No."

She nods and jots something down in her notes.

"Are you writing down that I'm a little dramatic in my break downs?" I ask, desperately trying to deflect.

She totally ignores my wit. "Did the near-kiss trigger a memory connected with your attempted suicide?"

I nod.

"Has any doctor ever talked to you about PTSD?"

"You mean like what guys in the Army get when they come back from war?" I ask.

Dr. West nods. "While very common in soldiers, anyone who's suffered a traumatic event or experienced a loss can experience PTSD. The reason you hear about it more with soldiers is because, thankfully, more are coming forward and asking for help because of their time in combat. But victims of a shooting, someone close to them dying, an accident, or a victim of rape can suffer from PTSD."

I flinch when she says rape.

"So, you think I have PTSD?"

"I can't say for sure. We'd have to diagnose that. But if a guy trying to kiss you triggered memories—a bad memory that turned into a panic attack—then it's a possibility."

"Can I get rid of it?" I ask, because the times when I can't control my body or my reaction is terrifying.

"For right now, I want to teach you how to cope and some more ways to combat a panic attack."

At this point, I'll take whatever I can get to gain a sliver of control back.

"There are a couple of techniques. For now, what I'd like you to try is focusing on physically touching something. Whether it be your jeans or shirt, or if you're barefoot, the ground underneath your toes. While you focus on whatever you're touching, I want you to take deep breaths in through your mouth, filling your chest."

It's hard to believe that will help, but I'm running out of options and I don't want to feel like I did in the shower. "Will this stop me from breaking mirrors?" I ask.

"That's the plan."

Good.

"And Tori? I'm proud of you."

"For what? Freaking out and breaking a mirror?"

Her eyes soften. "For getting away from a situation that made you uncomfortable. For telling me what happened. You're stronger than you think."

But am I really? Because I doubt it.

13

I slip into auto shop. I've managed to move through school today without anyone noticing me. After the incident at the tracks a couple days ago, I dreaded the stares or questions. The door opens again and it's like Nick has a tracking beacon on me. His eyes immediately find me, and he heads straight for where I'm sitting.

"Are you feeling better?" he asks as he sits across from me at our table.

"Huh?"

He gestures to my stomach. "From Friday night at the tracks. Dani said you were feeling sick."

They all thought I was sick? I silently thank Dani for covering for me. "Oh. Yeah, much better."

He nods his head but looks me over like he's trying to decide if I'm still sick or not. "Doug was upset."

"Okay...?" I could care less about Doug, but I don't say that. I don't want to deal with questions that would come from it.

"You know he likes you, right?" he asks.

Fanfreakingtastic

"I'm guessing the feeling isn't mutual?"

Not even a little bit. "Your guess would be correct."

He hesitates and then looks around the room. In a much quieter voice he asks, "Is it because you like girls? Because that's totally cool, too. I don't judge."

My head jerks back. Wasn't expecting that.

"Umm, thanks for the non-judgmental stance, but no, I'm not a lesbian."

He looks so puzzled. "I don't get it."

"Get what?" Now I'm the one who's confused.

"Why won't you give Doug a shot?"

I don't get why he's pushing this. Am I automatically supposed to like Doug because he's showing interest? Is Nick just trying to help his buddy out?

"I want to be a nun," I say with a serious face.

"What?!" And that gets the attention of the whole class.

"Calm down, would you," I wave my hand in front of his face. "I'm just kidding. I'm not even Catholic. I just don't want to date anyone right now. Okay?"

He slouches back into his seat like he didn't nearly leap out of his chair a second ago. "Oh, sure. I get it. I can respect that."

I raise a brow at his suddenly chill demeanor. "Can we get back to the project now?"

"The project? Really?"

Why does he look so surprised? Are we going to have a gossip session? "Did you want to talk about *your* love life?"

He bursts out laughing, causing more stares. A small smile touches my lips. "No, that's okay," he says in between gasping for breaths.

"You get to dig into mine, but I don't get the same pleasure?" I ask, and I can't believe I'm teasing him right now. I haven't teased a guy in a really long time.

"Well, as a wise person said, 'I don't want to date anyone right now. Okay?'"

I give him a mock bow. "Touché."

He looks down at his paper and clears his throat. "You'll let me know if that changes?" he asks, the laughter gone from his voice.

I swallow, hard. "If what changes?"

"If you...uh...you know, feel like dating?"

Dating. Just one word, one terrifying, panic-inducing word.

"I don't think—" I start.

"Forget I asked."

Wow, I think I hurt his feelings. He looks everywhere but at me. I lean a little closer and lower my voice. "I'm not someone you would want to date. I..." How do I tell him that I'm so messed up that I'll only bring pain and disappointment? That the idea of dating anyone makes me physically ill? Hence why I fled on Friday night.

"Let's just settle on friends. Sound good?" he asks.

This guy. He keeps saving me with an easy out.

"Sure." I hope that sounds convincing, because I'm not sure how much of a friend I can be right now. Putting aside the fact that he's a guy, I'm sucking in the friends' section of life.

"All right, wow, super awkward. How about this project on our engine, huh?" I could hug him for changing the subject. "You're probably going to need to come to my house soon."

"Okay."

I'm not really listening to Nick as he goes over what we need to do next on the project. The earlier levity is gone, but I'm so thankful he's able to roll with it. He starts pointing out things we need to do. But my mind drifts to a world of 'what-ifs'. What if last year hadn't happened? What if my mom never found me? What if the thought of a guy taking me out didn't terrify me? What if I let someone in? So many 'what-ifs.' It makes my mind drift to the end of my last appointment with Dr. West.

"*That past is set,*" *she says.*

"*I know.*" Man, do I know that.

"*Sometimes we let ourselves drift into this world where we play out scenes again and again. We dissect every moment. We let the guilt weigh us down. We let the knowledge we've acquired shame us.*"

"*How do you not, though? How do you not think about the ways life could be different?*" My heart begs her to answer these questions.

"*You see the past. See it, live it, and learn from it. Learn that tomorrow is a chance for a fresh start. Nothing is permanent. Change is the only constant we have in this life. Change however you want. It'll take time. But instead of counting the what-ifs, grab on to the what-nows. Grab onto them with both hands. What do I want now? What do I want to change now? What am I willing to do now?*"

"*I don't know if I can,*" I say in a quiet voice.

"*That's okay. You're being honest with yourself. That's one of the hardest things to do and one of the most important. As long as you stay honest with yourself, we can work on the rest. I want you to go home and think about what you want now. I know that's vague, but it's just to get you thinking. And remember: this is what you want; not your parents, not me, no one but yourself.*"

"*Okay,*" I whisper. I can give that a shot.

14

Should I?

I've been staring at my closet door for the past hour. I haven't been able to get back in there since the night the mirror broke last weekend. It's Tuesday—the first day my mom hasn't been constantly sticking her head into my room to check on me.

I'm dying to go dig around up there some more. Is it wrong to poke around in someone else's things? Like what if he shows up and wants his stuff? I bite my lip and drum my fingers against my thighs. Technically this is my room now and he left all this stuff. So, it's not like a real invasion of privacy. Right?

I surge to my feet and limp a little to the closet. Thankfully the cut wasn't too bad. I run my hand over the wall, searching for the little knob on the hidden panel. My fingers catch and I ease it open. Hopefully wherever Mom is in the house she can't hear me. I climb the ladder to the hatch overhead. It gives a groan as I push it open. I stop and wait to see if the noise carried. No knock comes at my bedroom door from my mom, so I climb the rest of the way into the attic.

Sunlight streams into the room, causing the dust I disturbed to float in the air. I flip the light on, flooding the room with more light.

I gravitate toward the images on the wall; I didn't get a good look at them last time. I didn't know a pencil drawing could look so lifelike. My hand hovers over the image of an unfinished car. I wonder if this is the one Nick and I are going to be working on. Zack took such time to draw this—how could he just leave Nick and their dream?

A sketch of Nick laughing catches my eye, and I smile. He caught Nick's essence perfectly. Always happy, smiling; so full of life.

The smile drops from my face. Someone like me would be toxic for him. I'd make that light in his eyes die. That's what I do. All I have to do is look at my mom.

I run my hands through my hair. "Get it together, Tori," I whisper to myself. "No more what-ifs."

I walk away from the picture of Nick and the sense of failure it brings, and head toward the desk with small steps. The wood groans a little. I'm not going to be able to stay up here for much longer. It's only a matter of time before Mom breaks down and checks on me.

I sit down at the desk and when I scoot closer to it, my feet bump up against something that gives a little. *What on earth is that?* I bend down and peer into the shadows. A small cardboard box sits there; I must have missed that the last time. I ease it out. It's taped, with Nick's name on the top. Part of me really wants to open it up, but it just doesn't feel right doing that. I'm already invading so much of Zack's privacy. Some day when Zack comes back, he can give it to Nick. I push it back and instead turn to the art journal I found a few nights ago. I thumb through the pages and stop on the same self-portrait of Zack I saw before. Everyone always talks about what a happy guy he is. But in this piece—he's broken. It's as if his face is fractured into tiny little shards. And his eyes—I have to turn my head away for a moment because of how much it feels like a punch to the gut to see something so familiar. "No one really knows us, do they Zack?" I ask the shattered portrait of him.

Tears roll down my cheeks as I trace the jagged lines. If I could draw, would I draw myself like this? Would I show the broken spirit within, like he does? Would my eyes look to the distance, pleading for a savior that I'm not sure can help me?

A sob catches in my throat. I rest my elbows on the desk and drop my face into my palms. Dark feelings crash into me, knocking the breath out of me. "Make them stop," I plead into the stillness of the attic.

Phantom hands grip my arms and then slither down my body. I grip my hair as images flash across my mind.

The deserted parking lot at the hidden soccer fields.

The lone orange streetlight barely reaching us.

Fog on the windows.

"No," I whisper.

My hands shake. And I can feel the constant pull of the spiral of my mind, like it's waiting to drag me down into a pit that I don't know if I'll come out of. I try to think of what Dr. West told me to do, but her words are scattered from my brain.

The insistent ringing of a phone breaks through the fog of my mind. I latch on to the sound like it's a tether, trying to find my way out of the abyss of memories I'm trapped in. The more I focus, the more I realize it's coming from my back pocket. I throw all my attention at the sound and bit by bit, I'm not back in that car but standing in a dusty attic.

The ringing stops and then my phone pings from my back pocket. I pull it out and check the screen. Dad.

Dad: Don't forget your appointment with Dr. West today.

I drop my head back and look at the ceiling, thanking whoever is listening for throwing me a lifeline.

* * *

"Something happened," Dr. West says, not even bothering to phrase it as a question. And I can feel the weight of her stare as she studies my face.

My eyes stay focused on the diploma behind her desk.

"You told me last week that you're tired of the way you're living. I can't help you if you won't talk to me."

My gaze slowly drifts from the diploma to her face. Nothing but patience shows in her eyes.

"Some days the dark pushes out all the light," I tell her softly.

"What were you doing when then dark seeped in?"

The image of Zack's drawing crashes into me again. I rub at the cuff on my left wrist. "Does anyone ever really know a person? Will anyone want them if they know all the dark and scarred parts of them? Will it always feel like I'm tainted? And will I ever stop infecting those around me?" My stomach clenches and my heart speeds up.

"I destroy things. People. Look at my mother. She's barely a glimpse of her old self. I flinch when someone tries to touch me. I'm toxic. I'm crumbling. I feel the nothingness right under my feet. And that tug that comes some days to just be done. And at times...it's so strong."

"What happened today?" she asks again.

I run my hands through my hair. "I found a door in my closet that leads to the attic. The guy that lived there before me—Zack— he left all his artwork up there. He's so talented. But I found one he did of himself. And it just resonated with me. Everyone describes him as this happy guy. But this picture, it's like he would know exactly how I feel. How is that even possible?"

"I'm so proud of you right now," she tells me.

"What?" I ask in complete disbelief.

"You just opened up to me about how you saw yourself in

Zack; telling me these things is important. You can't expect life to change if you aren't willing to talk to me. I'm going to tell you things that you might not believe right now, but I'd like you to listen."

I nod once, not knowing where this is going.

"You didn't destroy your mom."

I open my mouth to argue, but she holds up her hand. "No, please, just listen. Did your mom make you slit your wrists?"

"No," I tell her, a little horrified at the question.

"We make our own decisions. However your mom is acting right now, that's her decision. We all make choices. We all have the agency to pick how we're going to react. Her choices are on her, never on you."

The sting of tears hit my eyes, but I don't let them fall. I'm tired of crying.

"It's going to take a while for you to come to terms with that. But everyone makes their own decisions, and they are wrong if they try to put those on someone else."

I choke down the emotions threatening to drown me.

"As for that dark pit, we're going to find a way out, together," she tells me.

"Is there a way?" I ask—or rather, plead.

"There's always a way. Have hope, Tori. Hold on to the hope of a better day. Hold on to it when you don't know what else to grasp on to. And don't you dare let go, because you've already lived the worst day of your life and you're still here fighting."

My dad's car idles outside of Dr. West's office and I quickly slide into the front seat to escape the cold. There's this tenseness in the car, like a palpable presence. And it wrecks me, because we never used to be like this, but this is how life is now.

"Do you—" Dad starts, then stops.

I look at his taut face. His eyes may be trained on the parking lot, but I'm not sure he even sees it. "Do I what?" I ask him.

His hands wring the steering wheel. "Do you think...does she feel like a good fit for you?"

"Dr. West?" I ask.

He dips his head.

"I think so," I tell him honestly.

He takes a large breath, his barrel chest expanding even more. "It's just, you seem so drained when you come out of there. I don't want this to make things worse."

Worse? Like when he had me locked up in that freaking mental health place? I take a deep breath, pushing down the anger threatening to surge out. He's trying, so I need to try too. "Dad, I used to try and not feel anything. Feeling again is draining. I've been numb for so long. I think if I'm feeling the bad stuff now it's because I tried for so long to block it out."

He takes several deep breaths. "I just want you to be happy again."

"Me too," I whisper.

Even though trudging through the feelings and thoughts with Dr. West make me feel worse at times, I do want to be happy again. I want that feeling joy brings, but it's been so long, I'm not sure I would even recognize it right now.

And I don't know if he realizes that I'll never be the daughter he used to have. I'm not going to be that peppy voice in the house. She died. And I'm trying to figure out who is climbing out of the ashes.

"So, uh, how 'bout the weather we're having?" he asks, breaking the awkward tension.

"Great segue, Dad."

He shrugs. "I try."

I lean my head against the window, letting the cold bite into my skin. "It's better than when you used to ask me if I kissed any boys."

The car jerks to the right for a second before he corrects it. "Do I need to worry about that?"

"No," I say, and a gust of air escapes his lips at my answer. "But don't worry. I'll let you know when you should start getting comfortable with the idea of being called Grandpa."

He coughs and I pat him on the shoulder. "That better not be for another ten years," he finally says.

"But you'd be a good-looking grandpa."

"That, I will not deny," he says, all smug.

A small smile creeps out and his face mirrors mine. I didn't realize how much I missed our easy banter.

We pull into the driveway and I catch a glimpse of my mom peeking through the curtains. Whatever lightness we were just feeling is quickly cast away.

His gaze follows mine. "Just give her time."

"You keep saying that."

"I know, Sweets, but that's all I can give you right now. And that's what you need to give her."

We get out of the car and head for the now-open door where my mom waits for us. Her face is twisted into an overly cheerful smile and she wrings her hands. I haven't really talked to her since the night I busted my mirror.

We all shuffle into the house, and I head toward the stairs.

"Did you have a good meeting?" she asks before I can disappear.

I stop on the first step and turn to her. "It was helpful."

Her body sags. "Good; that's good," she says, more to herself than me.

I trudge up the stairs. "Dinner's in an hour," my dad calls after me.

"Okay," I yell back down.

I shut myself into my room and sink into the softness of my bed. Talking with Dr. West is exhausting and freeing all at once. But feeling again kind of sucks.

My phone buzzes in my pocket.

Nick: want to come over tomorrow after school to work on the project?

My first reaction is to cringe and say no. But at the same time, I know I'm stuck in this class, and I can't fail. The thought of going to his house fills me with dread, but is that how I'm going to live forever? When do I get to stop being terrified all the time?

Me: sure

One word, but I doubt he'll ever know how hard it was to type —how hard my fingers shook as I typed each letter in.

Nick: k, I'll see you at 4

Nick: and be ready to work and get your hands dirty

I hope he realizes that he's going to be doing most of the work or we're going to bomb this project.

Me: no promises

15

I STAND AT THE BASE OF NICK'S PORCH STEPS AND I'M WAVERING. I know we need to work on this project, and the car is at his house so there's no way around that, but I can't shake the feeling I'm crossing some invisible line. This shouldn't be that big of a deal, and yet I'm going to be alone with a guy. And that right there is making my insides twist into a knot I'm not sure I know how to untangle.

I can do this. I've lived through some garbage days; this is nothing. I keep trying to hype myself up as I put one foot on the bottom step, but before I can go any farther Nick's voice halts my progress.

"In here, Tori," he calls from the garage. "Hurry up inside. All the warm air is escaping."

I slowly follow his voice into the large garage. Bright florescent lights flood the place. Tools are scattered around the floor next to a pretty rough-looking car. The paint is chipped everywhere and it's missing a side mirror. How long is it going to take to finish this thing?

The garage door starts to lower, and I fight the need to run. It stops a good two feet from the bottom, and I know that I'll have no problem squeezing out if I panic.

"So, here's the engine. I know it doesn't look like much, but it will when we're done," he says, and I turn toward him. He walks away from the garage door button and stands next to the engine that's been hoisted out of the car. "And don't worry; I'm going to show you what to do. It'll be easy."

Well, he has a lot more faith in me than I do.

He points to a low stool and I plop down onto it. "Okay, first we need to clean these parts." He motions to a tray filled with bits of metal that I'm assuming make up an engine. "Heads up, we're gonna be working with some harsh-smelling stuff."

He hands me a rag and a bottle that says Oil Eater on it. This is going to destroy my hands. "Just dab a little on the rag and start rubbing."

I open up the bottle and immediately shove it away. "What. Is. That? It smells like something that crawled out of the sewer and died."

Nick bursts out laughing. "It's just a cleaner."

"Well, it's awful. Wait—is this going to make us sick and pass out from the fumes?" My eyes dart back to the almost closed garage door.

He puts the cap back on it. "Not if you close the bottle. But I've also got fans in the corner too if we need them."

I lean forward on my stool and gingerly pick up the cloth that fell to the floor. "Are you seriously afraid to touch it?" he asks.

"No, but that stuff *is* like toxic waste."

He chuckles and shakes his head. I start rubbing the pieces he hands to me while he works on his own. I scan the garage. Pictures of him hang on the wall next to us. He's standing by an old souped-up car; and on the other side is Zack.

"That's you and Zack, right?" I ask, pointing at the photo.

He looks over and a small smile graces his face. "Yup. We've always loved cars. We actually have a plan to take this car on a road trip when we graduate. Not sure if it'll happen though. I still can't believe he left without saying goodbye."

I don't get how Zack could've left without saying anything. Did his parents even let him? It sounds like he and Nick have been friends forever. Zack's parents have to know that. But maybe there's a lot of things that Nick doesn't know. Like, I wonder if he knows about that room in the attic. Does he know about those pictures? About how Zack portrayed himself in his art?

"That is kind of weird," I say after a bit.

His face pulls into a quick frown, but it clears just as fast. "Okay, we're really going to get dirty now. You might want to take off your cuffs," he says, reaching out and tapping them.

I wrench my arms away and hide them in my lap, causing him to freeze with his hand in midair.

"It's me, isn't it?" he asks softly, dropping his hand into his lap.

I search his face, trying to see where he's going with this. "Huh?"

"I feel like you can't stand me, and I don't know why."

Well, this is awkward. I don't even know how to explain any of this. I'm not even sure how I feel around him half the time. I don't detest *him*...just the uneasiness I feel around any guy. But trying to tell him any of this will just confuse him more.

"What do you mean?" I know it's a dumb question the moment it leaves my lips. And he does too, since he's basically calling me a liar with those eyes. "It's not you, it's me." I wince at the lamest cliché I could ever say.

He grabs his chest like I've wounded him. Such drama. "Ouch, you're the first girl to say those words to me."

I raise a brow at that load of bull. "Really? I highly doubt that."

He laughs and shakes his head. But the laughter is a short reprieve from the seriousness of the conversation.

"But seriously, did I do something wrong?" He's so sincere. I don't really sense any judgement from him.

I take a deep breath. I need to tell him something. And I realize quickly: I want to tell him something.

"No, I just don't like being touched. I like my personal space. Don't want my bubble invaded. So even though it sounds like I'm brushing you off, it really *is* me." That's only a fraction of the whole story, but it's more than I've told anyone—outside of Dr. West.

"Okay. I can respect that." He turns back to the engine, scrubbing at some piece of metal, but accepting my answer.

I didn't realize how much his response would affect me till right now. Most of my friends in Arizona stopped talking to me after everything. So many people gave me a wide berth, or looks filled with pity. I'm not even sure if any of them were sincere when they talked to me.

I release a huge gust of air. Thanking him in my mind for not pushing it.

He picks up another rag. "You should still take off the cuffs or they're going to get wrecked."

And that thankfulness is kind of short-lived, because he can't know what the cuffs are hiding. He can't see it. I look down, debating. The scars are still pink and really noticeable. Maybe he won't ask questions, but what if he does? What if he tells someone what he sees? I don't think I can handle everyone knowing.

"Do you have any gloves?"

He looks around the strewn-out tools. "I promise it'll just wash off with some soap. Are you afraid of getting it under your nails?"

Oh, thank goodness! He just gave me the perfect excuse. "Well, yeah. What girl wants grease under her nails? Actually, why would *anyone* want grease under their nails?"

Seriously, the more I think about it, the more that sounds gross and unsanitary.

"There is this thing called soap. It cleans stuff," he deadpans.

"I'd still rather not have to clean grease off," I tell him quietly.

He stares at my face and then moves his gaze to my cuffs and back again. "All right. Let me go see if my mom has some. It might be like dish scrubbing ones."

"That I can do."

Crisis averted. At least for now.

* * *

"How was it?" Dani asks as soon as I answer my cell.

"How was what?"

She huffs into the phone like it's a chore that I can't read her mind. "How was working with Nick?"

I want to tell her it wasn't as terrifying as I thought it'd be, but she wouldn't understand. "It smelled awful, but it was fine."

"Nick doesn't smell."

I laugh, picturing her face scrunched up and overly offended. "Not Nick—the stuff to clean the car parts."

"Oh. Well, that sucks. Did you guys talk about me?"

Ahh, the real reason for this phone call. I sag against my bed. "No, actually. We just mainly worked, and he told me what to hand him. Not very exciting." I pause, wondering how she's going to take my next question. "How come you haven't told him you like him?"

The line goes silent, and I pull the phone away to make sure she didn't hang up.

"Is it that obvious?" Her words seem straightforward, but her voice sounds like she's surprised that anyone could know. I'd bet ten dollars if I was there right now, she'd be biting her lip, looking extremely worried.

"I'm not sure, but I kind of got the impression you do" is what I tell her, but what I'm thinking is hell yes, it's obvious. I just moved here, and I've picked up on it right away. So, I bet everyone that knows her sees it too. She's not really subtle about it.

She sighs. "I'm not ready to tell him yet. Maybe you can sniff out some information," she says.

I groan into the phone. "Come on, Dani. What is this, fifth grade?"

"No, but you still could help me out and do it."

A year ago, this would not have been a problem. My friends and I did crap like this all the time. Now though? I barely handled being in Nick's garage and speaking, never mind trying to figure out who he likes. The last thing I need is for him to think that *I* like him. "I don't know. How about if he ever brings it up, I'll ask him?"

"Fine," she says. She's pissed, but talk about putting me in a super awkward situation.

"K, well, I'll see you in the morning. Bye," she says and then hangs up.

I toss my phone on my bed and flop back against the pillows. I might need to start finding a different way to school.

16

"Fingers still pretty?" Nick asks over his shoulder as I climb
into Dani's car.

I hold up my hands. "Yup, the gloves did their job."

He turns around, completely facing me. "Good," he says, and I
glimpse Dani rolling her eyes in the rearview mirror.

"We need to get together again soon to work on the written
part of the project. How 'bout I come over sometime this weekend?" he asks.

I watch Dani's hands tighten on the steering wheel as she pulls
up to a red light. My eyes dart back to him, but he's completely
focused on me. How can he not notice her reactions? "Yeah, that
should be fine," I hedge.

"All right, it's a date," he says, and turns back around.

Dani whips her head toward him. Ugh, could he have picked a
worse word to use? A car blares their horn at us. "The light's green,
Dani," Nick says.

Someone needs to have a talk with this guy. He can't be this
oblivious.

We pull into a parking spot at school and Dani gets out of the car, slamming the door in her wake. She marches away from us, her strides angry and loud. "What's up with her?" Nick asks, looking completely lost.

"You cannot be that dense."

"What?" he asks, his face scrunching up.

I don't want to do this. But he's got to know he's hurting her. And even though this is the last thing I want to be doing right now, enough is enough. Screw trying to be discreet. "She likes you," I tell him, exasperated.

"Well yeah, I like her too—we're friends." He shrugs like that's all there is to it.

I have the sudden urge to hit him with my backpack, but my hand will have to do. I smack him on the shoulder.

"Hey," he shouts, jerking back.

"She likes you as more than a friend," I tell him, but I leave out calling him an idiot.

He rubs at his shoulder. "Huh?"

I look at him, jaw dropped. "How can you not *see* that?" I ask.

He raises his hands in a helpless gesture. "I've known her since kindergarten. It never crossed my mind."

I blow out a breath. "Well, she's been getting mad at me because she thinks I'm making a play for you. No matter how many times I tell her we're friends and I don't want to date you."

He winces at my words, and I realize how cutting they sound.

"You know I don't want to date *anyone*," I tell him in a near whisper.

"I'm sorry she keeps getting mad at you," he says, ignoring my last statement.

"Do you like her as more than a friend?" I ask. And I don't want to think about why the answer really matters to me, because it does.

He rocks back on his heels, an annoying smirk taking over his face. "I don't. Why? Sudden change of heart?"

Stupid boy.

"You might want to tell her that," I say, not taking the bait.

"I'll figure something out," he says, but that's probably code for "I'm probably not going to do anything and maybe it'll go away."

"All right. See you later," I say.

"Don't forget I'm coming over tomorrow!"

I throw a hand up over my shoulder and walk up the stairs into school, heading straight for my locker, afraid that maybe Dani is going to be there, but she isn't. Regina is though.

"Hey," I say to her while I spin the dial, afraid to look at the judgement that's probably plastered on her face.

"Dani's pissed about Nick," she tells me without even a hello.

"I know, but she won't listen to me." My shoulders tense, waiting for her to lay into me.

"She won't listen to me, either," she says unhappily.

I finally get the courage to face her. She rolls her eyes at me. "Dani did the same thing with Doug about a year ago; none of us could even look at the guy. It's a little different with Nick. I think she just imagined that he'd always be there and eventually they'd be like high school sweethearts or something. But everyone can tell he doesn't look at her that way. It doesn't matter. She won't listen. She never does when it comes to guys."

"Why are you telling me this?" I ask.

"Because as secretive as you try to be, you wear a lot of emotions on your sleeve. I can tell that you're not interested in any guys right now. But I also get it with Dani. You're not the first friend she got pissed about when it came to some guy. Hopefully it'll pass. Just ride it out."

I guess I shouldn't be too surprised that I have an unapproachable vibe about me—especially after the incident at the tracks. But it unnerves me that I'm apparently transparent.

"Here's hoping," I tell her.

Regina gives me a sort of sad smile as the warning bell rings. "Let's get to homeroom," she says.

"Oh joy," I add. Can't wait to see who else witnessed that whole discussion between Nick and me. Or who Dani already talked to.

* * *

"Do you like Nick?" Britney asks.

It takes everything in me not to groan when I look up from the torture that is Algebra 2 and stare at her. Word spreads fast. Is everyone going to ask me this today? Homeroom was bad enough with all the stares. With such a small school, it didn't take long for word of Dani storming off to circle around. I can't even imagine what'll happen at lunch. I don't have the energy for this. "Excuse me?" I ask, even though I clearly heard her.

"I was wondering if you like Nick."

I shrug. "He's a nice guy."

I know what she's really asking, but I still feel like these are Danielle's friends and not mine. That fear of saying the wrong thing and causing all sorts of drama haunts my every step.

She raises a brow, clearly picking up on my dodging. "Yeah, he's nice, but do you want to go out with him?"

"No." My answer is quick and firm.

"Why not?" Her eyebrows scrunch down.

"I don't want to date anyone right now." How many more times am I going to have to say that? I feel like a broken record. I look down at my math work, hoping to end this line of questioning.

But Britney will not be deterred. She scoots closer, dashing any hope I had. "Was your last break-up bad or something?"

Images of *his* face bombard my mind, and it feels like a vice is closing around my neck. My voice drops to barely above a whisper. "You could say that."

"Oh?" She wants more. I can't give her that.

I clear the emotion from my throat a few times. "So, what answer did you get for number ten?" I ask.

I feel her eyes scanning me, even though I'm looking at the textbook. Thankfully, after a moment she looks down at her notes and we delve into math.

17

─────

The doorbell rings, and my mom pops into the living room like she's been waiting out of eyesight for this exact moment.

"Mom, you can go back in the kitchen."

"Nonsense. I've got to meet this guy."

I head for the door, still watching her. "Mom," I plead.

She raises a brow and gets comfortable leaning against the wall. Guess this is unavoidable.

I feel sick as I reach for the handle. "I can hear you guys. Just thought you should know," Nick calls from the other side.

Of course he can hear us. Awesome. My forehead thumps into the doorframe. "Are you hitting the door?" he asks.

Before he can say anything else, I pull the door open. Nick's smiling face greets me. "Come on in," I wave him into the house, my face probably red.

My mom stands up straight and Nick heads right for her. "You must be Tori's mom." He holds out his hand.

She grabs his hand. "It's so good to finally meet the boy I've heard so much about."

He looks over at me with a cocky smirk on his face. "Talking about me?"

"Please check your ego at the door."

"Tori," my mom says, horrified.

Nick laughs. "She's just kidding." I'm not really joking, but I'd rather not prolong this moment.

Mom looks between us, and I see that little glimmer in her gaze. I just know she's getting her hopes up. I'll have to squash that later. Maybe if I tell her about Dani, it'll bring her down gently. Last thing she'd want is some love triangle that involves her best friend's daughter.

"Well, I'll leave you guys to your schoolwork," she says with a little wave and walks out of the room.

"Let's just work here in the living room," I tell Nick. I have no desire for him to go up to my room, and the kitchen is too much of my mom's domain.

We sit on the couch and I pull my binder for auto off the coffee table. "Is it weird being here?" I ask him. I don't know why I didn't think about how odd it would be for him to be in Zack's old house.

He rubs his hand against the couch. "Yes and no. It's the same house that I've been to a million times. But the paint, the furniture, the vibe...it's all different. It's like seeing a memory in a dream—they're never the same there."

I sit in silence, not really knowing what to say. I've never experienced that, but I do know what he means about how memories change in our dreams. Mine just happen to be terrifying instead of nostalgic.

"No way," he says in complete awe.

I look up at him and his eyes are wide, his mouth hanging open. He's totally going to get a bug flying in there.

"What?" I'm suddenly real nervous on whatever has caught his attention.

"Do you have a cousin that looks exactly like you?"

Well, that's a weird question. "Uh, no."

His head swings back to me and he points at one of the many pictures on the mantle. "You were a cheerleader?" The way he says that, you'd think he was just plopped into an alternate universe.

I know what he sees in that photo. Decked out in my cheer uniform, hands on my hips, hair and makeup done to perfection, and a huge smile plastered on my face.

"I was."

He jerks his head back. "You have to give me more than that."

"Nope." I shrug.

"Come on, Tori. Please?" He's begging?

I huff out a breath. "Fine."

He bounces in his seat like he's five.

"I used to cheerlead at my old high school."

"And...?" he prompts.

I look at the photo on the mantle for a moment before glancing back down at my notebook. "I don't do it anymore" is what I tell him, but it's so much more than that. That girl died; she's not coming back.

I clear my throat and point at the notes for our project. "So, tell me what to add into our paper."

I feel him searching my face. I know my answer sucked, but...I just can't.

* * *

"And why don't you cheerlead anymore?" Dr. West asks.

"I'm not that girl anymore."

She sits across from me, waiting. This is her thing. Typically, the whole staring at me would annoy me, but she's giving me time to decide whether or not I want to talk more.

"Even if I was fixed like my mother wants, I don't think I'll ever be the girl she knew. That girl is gone."

"You're right, she is gone."

Whoa, she's agreeing with me. I kind of feel like celebrating. Maybe throwing my hands up in the air. Add in a good fist pump.

"Just like I'm not the same person I was in college. We all change. It's one of the few things you can count on in this life: change."

"Yeah. But change sucks."

Her face actually breaks into a small smile. "It can. But sometimes when we're living in a chaotic mess, we forget that we can change what we want," she says.

"What do you mean?"

"If you don't like how things are going, change it to something you want. You hate the song on the radio? Change the station."

I start to open my mouth, but she cuts me off. "I know you're going to say it isn't that easy. Of course it isn't. The things we want the most are usually the things we've got to work the hardest for."

"What if you don't want to work so hard?"

"I think you do; you're just scared. Fear has the ability to paralyze us. It makes us think that we can't succeed. You have to fight that fear. No one else can do it for you, but I'm here to give you the tools so you can."

"I'm not going to cheerlead anymore."

"Okay." A simple response, but said without judgement. I didn't realize I needed someone to be all right with that decision.

"Is there anything you'd like to do instead?" she asks.

"Oddly enough, I've enjoyed working on the car."

"Hmm."

"What? What's with the 'hmm'?"

"You never really seemed excited about auto shop before. Could this have anything to do with the partner you're working on the car with?" she asks.

"Really, Doc?"

She wiggles her eyebrows at me. "You never know."

"I don't know when I'll ever want to go down that road again," I tell her. All the levity from earlier leaving.

She nods slowly, her eyes never leaving mine. "Maybe that's something we can work on, but not now. For now, let's keep working on you. Okay?" she asks.

"Sounds good," I tell her.

18

"Two questions: what's the plan for tonight? And what's our plan for prom?" Regina asks.

I munch on my pretzels, hoping to stay out of this conversation. I honestly just want to crash and watch TV in my room instead of going out or going to prom.

Dani waves around a fry. I watch it, waiting for the ketchup to fall off of it and onto her. Part of me wants to warn her about it, but then again, she keeps being weird about Nick, so maybe she deserves to mar her perfect shirt.

"I just assumed we were going to the game," Dani says.

Wait, no, I'm not really sure I want to go to another basketball game. Last time did not end in a good way. "Are we going to haunted train tracks again? Because if so, I'm out," I tell them, secretly hoping they say yes so it'll give me an out.

"No, supposedly there's a party after the game," Doug says from a couple seats down.

Today is the first time he's sat with us again at lunch since the incident at the tracks. I thought it'd be weird to be around him, but since I'm not freaking out, it's easier. Plus, he hasn't tried to hit on me or anything, so that makes this a whole lot less awkward.

"Where?" Gretchen asks, bouncing in her seat. I *cannot* share in her excitement.

"At Rossi's," Doug says.

I shake my head back and forth. "No way in hell," I say.

"Why not?" Britney asks.

"Because he's a jerk," I say. And a creep who makes my skin crawl. Plus, he treats women horribly, and I have no idea why they don't see it.

"He's kind of gross," Dani says. "Plus, I bet he wouldn't mind getting her drunk. He's got a habit of doing that."

"Eww. No," I say.

The thought of what he could try makes the hair on my arms stand up.

Nick kicks my foot under the table. "Don't worry, Doug and I won't let anything happen to you. Plus, you better come to my game," he says, flashing me a smile and it makes me smile in return. I'm sure they would, but I don't know if I really want to put myself in that spot. Not to mention Doug and I don't have the best track record.

"You should come," Dani says, and I raise a brow at that. Lately it seems like she doesn't want me anywhere near Nick. But maybe I can help him *see* her and she can put the moves on him.

"We'll see," I say.

"That's as good as a yes," Regina says.

"Whatever," I say, but I follow it with a forced laugh.

* * *

"So, who are we playing?" I ask Regina as I sit next to her on the bleachers.

"Lyman Hall." She doesn't even look away from the court when she responds.

"Hey, Tori," Doug says as he slides in next to me.

And cue the awkwardness. "Hey."

He runs a shaky hand through his hair. "Can I, uh, talk with you for a minute?" he asks. He points to a spot besides the bleachers.

"Uhh..." Last time I was semi-alone with him it didn't turn out so well. Actually, it was pretty awful.

He puts his hands up in a pleading gesture. "I promise, just talking." His face is the perfect portrayal of innocence.

"Sure," I say, but I really don't want to. I'd rather just get up and walk the couple of miles home. Because I can't take another panic attack.

I get up to follow him, but before I step down, I catch sight of Nick standing on the sidelines watching us. I wave at him and he raises his chin. His mouth pulls into a hard line. I wonder what he thinks is going on here. I shake my head. Not sure why I even care about that.

I follow Doug to the back of the bleachers and we stand there facing each other. Anyone watching us has to see the uncomfortable vibe between us. It doesn't help that my hands keep shaking. I shove them in my pockets so it isn't too obvious. "What did you want to talk about?" I ask, needing to get this over with.

He blows out a large breath, stirring the hair hanging in his face. "I want to say I'm sorry."

Excuse me? "What?" I ask.

"I'm sorry for trying to kiss you."

Okay, wow, not what I expected. And I don't know what I would have done if he did kiss me. Even thinking about it turns my stomach sour.

"I just read the situation wrong, and I wanted you to know that I'm sorry if I've made it weird," he tells me.

"Thanks" is what I get out, but inside I'm still reeling. It's nice of him to come and apologize. Maybe if I was in a different place —a healthier one—in my life, I would have taken the kiss differently, but not right now.

"I like you, but I get it," he says.

I rock back on my heels, doubting that, but appreciating it nonetheless.

"Okay, not really, but I respect you enough to back off."

My voice sticks in my throat. "Thank you," I croak out. He has no idea how much it means to me for him to back off and respect me enough to do so. "I'm not someone who would be worth dating right now," I say. "But I can offer being a friend. Although I'm not sure if I'll be a good one." I'm being so honest with him, but he deserves it.

"That works for me," he says. He looks a little sad, but like Dr. West told me, I can't worry about his reaction—only mine.

We head back to our seats and Dani looks at me with big, hopeful eyes. They dim quickly, though, when she takes us in.

She grabs my arm and pulls me in close. "Well?"

My eyes narrow on her. "Did you know what he was going to talk to me about?" I ask her.

"He asked me if you liked him," she says.

"And what did you tell him?" I ask.

She shrugs. "I told him you might."

I rip my arm from her. "You had no right," I hiss at her. I walk away from her to sit on the other side of Doug.

"Everything okay?" he asks.

I take a deep breath, shaking off the annoyance gnawing at me. She probably hopes that if I get distracted with some guy, it will mean nothing is going down with Nick. "Don't worry about it. Let's just watch the game."

I face the court, and thankfully the ref blows his whistle and tosses the ball up in the center of the court for the tipoff.

My eyes drift until they find Nick. Someone passes him the ball and I watch as he dips and drives toward the net. His movements are fluid, his muscles tense, showing their definition. I never noticed how good of shape he's in. I didn't even bother to really pay attention during the last game. He goes in for a layup and sinks his shot. Everyone jumps from their seats screaming and stamping, including me and Doug. Nick points to our section and grins. Gretchen, Dani, and even Regina go nuts.

I smile watching them and turn back to see Nick wink at me.

"So, are you coming tonight?" Doug asks when everyone settles back down.

"To the party?"

"Yeah," he says.

I look at the court one more time, watching Nick smile. My eyes drift over to Regina and Gretchen's smiling faces. Maybe this night will be different. Maybe I could enjoy it a little. But I don't say any of that. Instead, I say, "Might as well. I don't have anything else going on."

19

Some new pop song assaults my ears before we even reach the front door. Who was allowed to pick the music? The front door opens, and two girls stumble out and down the stairs. One falls into the snow. Classy. "They're going to freeze to death," I mutter to Regina.

"They're the idiots that dressed like it's summer," she says.

A guy strolls out of the house and heads straight for them, laughing at the drunk girl who's still lying in the snow. Her friend's too busy laughing at her to bother helping her up.

"Come on, baby," the guy says as he lifts her up. I hope that's her boyfriend. I shudder, and not from the cold.

"Coming?" Doug asks from the front door.

"Yeah."

I shouldn't be here.

We walk into a scene that's eerily similar to what feels like a different life. Guess it kind of was. The bass of the loud music thumps in my chest, and most of the lights are turned off. Bodies grind on the makeshift dance floor in the living room. Every surface is littered with red plastic cups. I trail behind Regina into the kitchen. Little does she know that she's my human shield tonight.

A keg sits in a tub of ice and the counter is lined with bottles of liquor. Guys from school fill in the area. Some nod at me and I avert my eyes.

"Drink, ladies?" Rossi asks, holding the tap to the keg.

Gross. Of course we had to run into him right away. I hope no girl actually takes a drink from him. Guy probably spikes them.

"I'm driving," Regina says, grabbing my arm and heading for the fridge.

"You can have at least one," he says.

"Maybe later," she dismisses him.

"He gives me the creeps," she says as she opens the fridge. She grabs two Cokes out and hands me one. "He's totally the type to get you drunk just to sleep with you. Probably the only way that he can get laid."

I watch Rossi. He nudges one of his friends and points at a girl dancing. He rubs his hands together and heads her way. The uneasy feelings from earlier echoes through me. This is such a bad idea. Maybe we should leave.

We move to the edge of the dance floor. Regina sways to the music and I try to shrink into her shadow. "Ooh, boys from West-brook," she says, pointing to a group of guys in polos and boat shoes. "I'll be back." She stands a little taller and her hips sway as she walks over to them.

I scan the people "dancing" and spot Doug with his hands gripping a blonde. He moves on quickly. Thank goodness.

A cheer goes up suddenly, mixed with a few groans. I stand on my toes trying to see what everyone is staring at, and I catch a glimpse of Nick with a bunch of guys in the middle of the crowd. They must be cheering for the basketball team; it was an amazing win.

The crowd parts, letting them make their way further in. High fives and fist bumps are handed out. Nick looks around the room, scanning until his eyes land on me. He says something to the guy next to him, who slaps him on his shoulder, and heads for me.

As he makes his way closer, I'm flooded with nervousness. *Wait, why would I be nervous? It's just Nick.* But for some reason the look in his eyes is different tonight. Is he still riding the high from his win? I look around me, making sure there isn't anyone else he could be fixed on. Nope—his eyes are totally on me. He stops a few feet away, giving me my distance. Somehow he already reads me so well. "Congrats on the win," I say after a moment of awkward staring.

"Thanks," he says, his face splitting into a huge smile.

"So..." I drawl. It's been a while since I felt self-conscious around him.

He lets out a nervous laugh and brushes his hand through his hair. Why is it when guys do that it makes their hair look good, but if I did that I'd look like a monster?

"I'm glad you decided to come to the party," he says. "And the game."

Someone drunkenly stumbles into him, almost knocking them both down. He helps right the guy. "Yeah, I'm not sure how long I want to stay," I say.

"Not your scene?" he asks.

I watch the group of girls having a blast dancing with each other. I can't even count how many times after a football game I was doing the same thing. Sadness settles in. Some days I want that back, that carefree feeling. But I don't think I'll ever get it again. "Not anymore," I say at last.

He stares, probably waiting for more of an explanation probably, but I'm not feeling real charitable with information right now.

"I doubt you'd want to dance," he says.

"You'd be right," I tell him, watching bodies moving across the makeshift dance floor. I'm not sure I would call that dancing. I see Regina draped over some guy. Looks like she found her mark.

He keeps that easy smile on his face. "You want to go somewhere and talk?" he asks.

My body seizes. They never mean talk. They always want something else. Is that what he wants? Does he want me to go into a room with him? I rub my arms. Maybe I should just walk home.

"Relax," he says. "We can sit right over there on the stairs." He points to the stairs right off the living room.

My nerves loosen a bit. This is Nick. He's never done anything to make me think he'd...do anything. I nod. I'm too much in my head to really respond.

We make our way around the living room and walk up a few stairs before plopping down. I sit next to the railing so I don't have to worry about anyone bumping into me.

Being a few steps up gives us an advantage. We can see most of the people across the living room. Nick points to some stupid tricks people are trying to do. And then some guy in a pink shirt starts acting like he's going to break dance, and everyone starts cheering. But with the way he's swaying I highly doubt it will last. He works his feet back and forth and then moves around in a circle. He drops like he's going to do the worm, but his feet slip out from him and he face-plants into the hardwood floor. I wince at the sound of his chin slapping the unforgiving ground. "Oh, that sucks," Nick says from beside me.

I laugh because it really does. "What was he thinking?" I ask.

"He wasn't."

We both laugh as we watch his friends help him from the floor. As soon as he's standing, he raises his arms above his head like he just completed some great victory. "He's going to feel that tomorrow," I say, watching the guy dance around some more.

"Definitely."

We continue to watch people make absolute fools of themselves for the next twenty minutes.

"I love people watching," I say.

He nods. "Seriously! I've learned that we go to school with some interesting people. Did you see Dan rapping? Who knew?"

"I know! He never even says anything in auto," I say.

"What about Topher with the back flip?"

"That was cool, but dumb," I say.

His eyes widen like he can't believe that I didn't think it was as amazing as he did.

I groan. "Come on, he almost took that little redheaded girl out."

"I guess he got lucky," Nick says, but he seems reluctant to agree. "We still on for tomorrow night?" he asks.

"The project?" I ask.

He nods his head.

"Then I guess we are," I tell him, and he smiles.

We look back to the crowd and I spot Dani. She's weaving—more like crashing—through the crowd with Gretchen on her heels. She's got a red plastic cup in her hand, and liquid sloshes out of it. Crap. I tap Nick on the shoulder and point toward Dani. He swears under her breath. "She's going to do something stupid," he says.

We watch Rossi grab her by her hips and she just laughs. But I know that look on his face. I've seen it. My heart pounds and I grip Nick's arm. "You need to go get her," I tell him. "She's too drunk, and I don't think Gretchen is going to be much help. Just go get her. It's time to take her home," I say.

He stares at me for a heartbeat. I plead with my eyes. *Save her. Save her from something worse than the hangover she's going to have tomorrow.* He nods once and walks down the stairs. I pull out my phone and text Regina.

Me: time to go

I scan the crowd for her and find her on the couch with a guy, she checks her phone. I see the pout on her face.

Me: Dani is drunk

She looks to where Nick is trying to pull Dani away from the guy.

Regina: Yeah, this is going to get ugly. Too bad, this guy is hot.

She gets up from the couch and I walk down the stairs. Dani has her arms around Nick's neck. Rossi seems a little pissed until a pretty blonde walks by and he walks after her.

"Oh Nicky, I love you." Dani's words are more slurs than anything else.

"I love you too, but I think it's time to head out," he says, trying to move her to the door.

Her mouth pulls into a pout. "But I don't want to," she whines.

She leans in to kiss him, but he turns his face, letting her lips hit his cheek. She laughs loud, like a hyena, at the wet smear she leaves on his cheek. "Such a tease, Nicky," she says.

Regina rolls her eyes. "Hey, we're going to go party somewhere else," she says from beside me and I smack her. Another party is *not* what Dani needs right now.

She winks and mouths, "Go with it" to me.

Dani immediately perks up. "Where?" she asks, and Nick heaves a huge sigh.

"You'll see," Regina says.

We head for the door, but Dani stumbles and laughs as more beer spills out of her cup. Regina grabs the cup and passes it off to some guy. She better not get anything on me. The last thing I need is to come home smelling like beer and have my parents think I'm drinking now.

Nick scoops her up and we keep walking. "What about Doug and Gretchen?" I ask. I totally forgot about him.

"He's already out at the car," Regina says. "And Gretchen said she wanted to stay." She lets Nick walk in front of us. "This isn't the first time we've had to drag her drunken self out of a party," she says.

"Really?" I ask, shocked. I don't see her like that.

"Yeah; it's gotten a little worse lately. But if we tell her we're going to another party, she always falls asleep in the car. She usually spends the night at my house or Britney's. Her mom would murder her," she tells me.

I follow them out to the car. I take one last look at the house and Rossi comes out the door. "Hey! Why you guys leaving with Dani so soon?"

"Time to go, man," Nick says, turning to face Rossi with Dani still in his arm.

"Have fun with her, Nick," Rossi says, and when I look at him, his face morphs into the one that haunts me.

A shudder works down my body.

"Come on, Tori!" Regina shouts at me from her spot beside Dani.

I run to the car and hop in. And as the car pulls away, I sit on my hands to try and stop the tremors.

* * *

"So, you went to a party?" Dr. West asks.

"Yeah."

"From the sound of that response I'm guessing you didn't like it?"

"I used to go to parties like that a lot back in Arizona. It's what we did on the weekends. Especially after games."

"And now?"

I swear she knows what my answer is going to be though.

I let out a large breath of air. "People do things when they're drunk that they normally wouldn't do. Like one time I got in the bed of a truck with a bunch of these huge football players. I didn't think there was anything wrong with it, but my friend wasn't having it, so we left."

"What was wrong with being in the truck?" she asks and leans forward in her seat.

I throw my hands up in the air. "They could have done anything with me. I was so drunk and past the point of caring. That's how Dani was last night."

"And you didn't like how the guy looked at her?" Her question is genuine; she isn't trying to make me look crazy. She seems to really want to hear my answer.

"You hear on the news about people slipping things into someone's drink and totally taking advantage of them. There was that swimmer who raped that girl behind the dumpster. But what if those guys walking by hadn't seen it and stopped him? What would have happened to her? Would she have woken up behind a dumpster? Would she have lived to the next day?" My voice rises with each question.

No one was there for me. No one came and saved me. No one stopped anything. No one.

Tears start streaming down my cheeks. "I don't think I want to talk anymore today," I tell her.

"One more question?"

I look down at my hands balled up in my lap and nod.

"What did you feel when you saw everyone get Dani out of the house?" she asks.

I pause. Did I feel anything when they closed ranks around her? I hadn't thought about my feelings then; but now?

"Angry. Jealous, maybe. But isn't that wrong?" I ask her.

"No."

I look up from my lap, taken back by her one-word response.

"Your feelings are never wrong. They are yours and you can own them. I would rather have you feel something than not. So no, feeling anger or jealousy is not wrong. It's what you felt. And I'm proud that you can be honest admitting that."

I didn't have a Nick to scoop me up when everything fell apart. I didn't have a Regina standing by with a plan already in place. And I didn't have a Doug waiting with a car, ready to take us wherever without asking questions.

"Not going to ask why I felt that way?" I ask.

She shakes her head. "No. You'll tell me why when you're ready. I'm not going to force you to do anything you don't want to, Tori. I might push you a little, but it's because I know you can take it. I won't go past your limits," she says.

Well, I'm glad someone knows my limits. 'Cause I sure as hell don't feel like I can trust myself most days.

20

"WE'RE DOING RESEARCH TODAY," NICK SAYS, LEANING AGAINST HIS car in my driveway.

"Research?" Is he taking me to an auto parts store? Isn't it getting a little late for that?

"Yup, it's a surprise. Hop in so we can get going."

He slides into the driver's seat, but I haven't moved from my spot. I can't. The familiar tightness of my lungs alerts me to the panic attack's gaining momentum. I don't like not knowing where he's taking me.

The passenger window rolls down and he leans over the seat. "Come on, Tori, I promise it'll be fun. If it's not, I'll bring you right back home. I promise."

I try the breathing technique Dr. West taught me. *In for ten, out for ten.* Nick keeps his eyes glued to mine, patiently waiting. He sees more than I want him to.

The tightness lessens. I get in the car, praying that I won't regret this.

* * *

"Go-karts?" I ask, looking at the building in front of us.

The smile that breaks out on his face catches me off guard. It makes him look so young. "Yeah! Haven't you ever done this before?" he asks.

"Have you ever seen me drive a car?"

His smile drops. "No, I haven't. Don't you have your license?"

"Not yet." Kind of hard to get your license when you're locked up in a mental health facility. Plus, I think my mom's afraid that I'd drive a car off a cliff somewhere. But I doubt he wants to hear any of that.

He rubs his hands together, beaming at me. "Well, this is going to be interesting, but don't worry; you're going to love it."

We walk up to the line to wait for our turn. Thank goodness we're inside because I think I'd freeze otherwise. Little go-karts zip by us, whipping my hair into my face. Nick raises his hand to brush it back, but I step away, letting his hand fall. He just rolls with it like it's not a big deal.

"So, uh...how's Dani doing today?" I ask him, trying to cover any awkwardness.

"She texted me saying that she didn't remember last night, but with how much she threw up this morning she never wants to drink again. Typical Dani."

"Does she get drunk a lot?"

"Not a ton, but enough that her text wasn't surprising."

We move forward in line until it's our turn. "Do I need to tell you which one is the gas and which is the brake?" he asks, changing the conversation.

I look up expecting to see a mocking smile, but he's totally serious. I squash the sarcastic retort bubbling out of my mouth. "I think I can manage. I may not have my license, but I did get my permit." And I haven't driven since then, but that's beside the point.

The smell from the exhaust envelops me as I slide into the

driver's seat and buckle my seat belt. Nick jumps into the kart next to mine. "You ready for this?" He's practically vibrating with excitement in his seat.

The light turns green and he lets out a loud whoop. I lurch forward, a little unsure, and try to follow behind Nick. Soon I'm flying down the track. Wind whips at my hair. And even though I'm probably not going very fast, it feels like I'm soaring.

The track curves and I slow to a crawl. Last thing I want is to crash. Nick races by me; pretty sure he just lapped me. "Keep up, Tori!" he screams.

I hesitate and then put my foot down on the gas. I surge forward again. The next curve appears and instead of slowing this time, I grab the steering wheel with a death grip and go for it.

My kart bumps the rubber sidewall a little, but I shoot around the curve. Adrenaline floods my veins. And a smile spreads across my face. This is freaking amazing!

Nick keeps ahead of me, but at least he's not lapping me again. We take a couple more trips around the track until the light turns red.

I pull my kart behind Nick's. He's standing beside his, a huge smile on his face. I jump out and run toward him. "So?" he asks.

"That was amazing," I tell him. I'm just about dancing on my toes with the leftover adrenaline coursing through me.

He bumps his shoulder with mine. "I don't think I've ever seen you with this much enthusiasm."

"I can't remember the last time I had this much fun," I say. And I'm being honest. It's been way too long since I enjoyed anything.

"Want to do it again?" he asks, his voice tinged with hope.

"Hell yeah!"

He laughs and leads the way to the back of the line.

* * *

"So, you went on a date?" Dr. West asks.

My heart constricts at the idea.

"Uh, no. Definitely wasn't a date," I tell her.

"Are you sure?"

Am I?

"Wouldn't I know if it was a date? He said it was research for our project. Plus, I told him that I don't want to date anyone right now. I'm barely capable of having friends," I tell her.

I hope Nick doesn't think that was a date. What if he did? Damn. Last thing I need is more drama, especially with Dani.

Dr. West leans back in her chair. "I know why dating might be hard. But why is it hard to have friends?"

"Doesn't every suicidal person have trust issues?" I ask with a lot of snark in my tone.

"Not necessarily," she answers calmly, not taking the bait.

I purse my lips, debating how to answer. "Friends want to know too much," I settle on. "And I'm not ready for that."

"Thank you for answering honestly. And it's okay that you're not ready, but don't use that as a shield. Sharing our darkest times with people can bring in more light than we ever imagined," she says.

I hear those words, and I want to follow them, but it's terrifying. And I don't know how Dr. West is able to wrangle that honesty out of me. But I guess if I'm going to be honest with anyone, therapy would be the place to do it.

21

"DID YOU HAVE A GOOD TIME THE OTHER NIGHT WITH NICK?" MY mom asks.

I turn from looking in the fridge for breakfast and see her standing in the doorway of the kitchen, her face awash in her perpetual mask of hope.

"Actually, yeah. Who knew driving go-karts would be so fun?" I tell her.

"Good," she says, but it's more to herself than to me. She walks the rest of the way into the kitchen. "Do you want French toast?" she asks.

I pause where I'm standing. Before, we used to have French toast every Sunday morning. It was our tradition. But it's been at least a year since that's happened. My first instinct is to say no, but I squash that. A precipice looms before me. I can feel it. I'm not sure what it means, but my mind tells me that this decision is important. "Yeah, that sounds good," I finally tell her.

A genuine smile gives light to her face that has been shadowed for a year. "Get the bread for me?"

"Sure."

I reach for the bread and hand it toward her. She traces my face with her eyes. Whatever she finds makes her smile even brighter and she turns back to the stove.

I decide to hop up on the counter to watch like I used to and take in the smells that wrap around all my favorite childhood memories. "So, how's your project with Nick going?" she asks, her voice hesitant.

She's trying and I guess it's my turn to try too. "Okay, but I don't know how much help I really am. Cars aren't really my thing."

She hums. "I'm sure you're pulling your weight. You've never been one to slack off," she says with conviction.

My throat tightens. I doubt she realizes that that's the first compliment she's paid me in such a long time. And all the motivational posters don't count. It's not like she reads them out loud to me—anymore. Besides, I ignore the posters in general. But ever since she found me in the bathroom, it's like she thinks I'm made of glass and the wrong touch will shatter me again. For a while that was true, but it hasn't been that way for some time.

"Thanks," I whisper.

"Do I smell French toast?" Dad asks from the doorway.

"Yup." Mom flips the bread.

My dad gives me a thumbs-up with a dorky smile. You would think I cured cancer, not agreed to breakfast.

He walks up behind my mom and snakes his arms around her waist. "Missed these Sunday mornings," I hear him whisper into her ear.

"Me too," she whispers back.

Guilt washes over me, but I push it back. I won't ruin this. It finally feels like maybe, just maybe, we can get back to some sort of normalcy. I don't know what that is now, but anything is better than feeling like a stranger within my own family.

"Set the table?" she asks me. I hop down and start grabbing plates and forks. I watch my parents out of the corner of my eye.

My dad rubs Mom's lower back, and she leans into him. There's no tension there. No hesitation on either part.

At least some things don't change. I might have forever altered our family, but I didn't ruin their marriage.

"We're going to Westport today. Did you want to come?" she asks.

I set down the plates on the table. "No, you two go. I'll stay home," I say without looking at her. She's probably disappointed, but I don't get the house to myself that often. And I've been dying for a chance to get back into the attic.

I drop down into my seat, and they join me at the table.

"Oh, well, okay. If I see anything cute, I'll send you a picture."

My dad kicks me under the table. I turn my head toward him, but he's solely focused on staring at his bacon. Seriously?

"Sure, Mom, that sounds great," I say.

A smirk spreads across Dad's face. I really want to kick him back.

"Good. Oh, Kris and Dani are coming over tonight," my mom says.

Ugh. No. "Why, Mom?"

She raises a hand to stop whatever else is about to come out of my mouth. "She's been my friend for years. And she's going through a tough spot right now. And while that doesn't excuse her behavior, I know she feels bad about the last dinner."

Yeah, I'm not so sure about that.

"Just give her another chance."

Perfect.

✳ ✳ ✳

I make my way back up the ladder into the attic. The desk calls to me this time. I bypass all the pictures and drawings and sit down in the chair. I push the art journal to the side and look at everything scattered about. Pencils, half-done drawings, and trash litter the space. I pour over the half-done drawings. Wilted flowers, the phrase *nothing lasts forever*, the word *escape*, all appear on the papers. Some of them are smeared with what could have been... tear drops? I pull open one of the drawers and a prescription bottle rolls to the front of the drawer.

I pick it up and note Zack's name on the bottle, along with the medication's name: Lexapro. He was taking an anti-anxiety drug? The bottle is half full. Why would he forget these? You're not supposed to stop taking them. The doctors who prescribed mine made sure to tell me that at least twice a day. I snoop through the drawer underneath. It's filled with blank paper. Another drawer is filled with pens and pencils. Except, at the back is a scrap of paper. Maybe it's a small drawing. I pull it out. Nick's name is on it beside a website with a password. What is this?

I need my laptop. I put my phone into my pocket and leave the attic. Back in my room, I grab my computer and sit on my bed and boot it up. I type in the address and a box pops up for a password. I start to enter it, but I stop myself. Why does this feel wrong? I mean, it's not like Zack lives here anymore. He left it behind. It can't be that important if he just left it in his desk, right? I finish entering the password and go to put the paper on my nightstand, but it flutters to the floor. I'll grab it later.

The only thing on the site is a video. Weird. Maybe it's about the car they were working on. I click play. Zack sits still, looking straight into the camera. From the looks of it, he's up in the attic. His eyes lack any warmth. They're bloodshot like he's been crying. His hair is a mess, and not in a good way. His shirt collar looks like he's tugged it a few times. What am I watching?

A cold hand of dread grips my spine like a vice.

"Hey, man. I've got to tell you some things."

I watch him visibly swallow, and the hair on the back of my neck stands up. "I don't think I can do this anymore." It's like he has to force the words past his lips. "With Britney deciding she doesn't want anything to do with me, my parents constantly fighting, and the threat of military school. Let's not forget my messed-up brain."

He rubs his hands across his face. "I haven't been good for a while. My doctor gave me some pills, but I don't like how they make me feel, so I just stopped taking them last week. I tried smoking pot, but it's not helping at all. Alcohol only numbs me for a little while. And when I sober up, it's like everything is out of control and I can't hold on. I'm just tired. I'm tired of this battle. I think that my parents would be better off if I wasn't here anymore. They always fight about me. About what I'm doing, what I'm *not* doing. My mom found an empty bottle of vodka in my room and that sent her through the roof. Dad was just mad because I took it from his stash. But how can I tell them I just don't want to deal anymore?"

He looks directly into the lens of the camera, and I know what he's about to tell Nick in this video. My heart shatters because I'm looking at me. I'm looking at the pain I've seen reflected in the mirror too many times. I'm looking at a kindred spirit. And I'm looking at what's going to crush Nick.

"So, I guess because you're the only one that really cares about me, I just want to tell you that I love you, man. I'm sorry that we won't be taking that road trip together, but I've had enough. Anything that's mine is yours. Not that I have much, but I bet there's some pictures up here that you'd want. And I want you to know that this has nothing to do with you. Don't mourn me. Hopefully I'm going someplace a lot better than here. It's got to be because I'm already living in Hell; can't imagine an eternity of this."

Tears stream down his face now, following their earlier tracks. "I just keep screwing things up." His voice breaks. "I keep making Britney cry. My mom, too. That dark abyss has been calling me for a long time and I can't resist that pull anymore. I'm too tired. Don't worry. I'll be in good hands. And I'll miss you, but it's for the best. There's a big envelope up here in the attic, filled with letters. They're in a box under my desk. Deliver those for me, would ya? They each have a piece of my heart for you guys."

He stops talking and just stares at the camera for a minute. Every emotion passes across his face and I'm not sure if he realizes that. I see the broken boy that wants love from his parents. The boy that wants the love of a girl and feels like he won't ever be enough for her. The broken person in front of me. So much like the picture he drew, so much like the person I see in the mirror. This is what it looks like to feel as if you've lost everything; like there's nothing left to live for.

I'm crying now. I want to jump through that screen and tell him that there are ways to keep that darkness at bay. That he doesn't even realize the hurt and torment he's leaving behind. The hearts that will be crushed, the lives that will be changed. But then again, I didn't think about that at all. I didn't think about how my actions really affected my mom and dad. How I helped break this family. I know Dr. West says that I need to let go of the guilt, but how? My choice brought us here. My choice is the reason my mom can't have a real smile. My choice is what moved us across the country.

I watch Zack through my tears, connected by our brokenness to a guy I've never even met, and it hits me. No one knows he killed himself. No one knows he's dead.

How? How does no one know? How was this kept hidden? Where are his parents? What did they do with his body? And Nick...this is going to kill him. This video is for him and he's going to have to live with this knowledge. I can't be the one to break him. I can't be the one to take that shining bright star and extinguish it. I can't crush him. I don't want him to be like me.

Zack's voice pulls me back to the computer. "My parents will find me tomorrow. Do great things, man. Make me proud. I'll be watching you and cheering you on. Don't mess up. And make sure you finish that car for me. Love ya, man."

This feeling coursing through me...is this what my friends felt like? Is this why none of them talked to me after the fact? Did they even get why my parents made us move away? The guilt knocks the wind out of me. But I don't think I had any friends like Zack had in Nick. I don't think there was anyone who would have missed me like I know Nick is going to miss him. Even now I'm not sure anyone would care enough. Dani is constantly mad at me because she thinks I'm making a play for Nick. No matter how many times I try to tell her I'm not interested.

I push my computer away from me like the bomb it is. If anyone sees this, the disaster it's going to leave in its wake will be awful. But how can I not tell Nick? How can I keep this from him? I keep picturing his face. The light and joy that shines forth from him.

Maybe I should ask Dr. West what to do. No, she would tell me to show Nick. And I'm not ready for that. I flop back on my pillow. I can't believe how much I have in common with Zack. He was much better at hiding it than I am, but I used to be that happy person that everyone thinks he was.

What a mess.

I can't be the one to make Nick's light go out. I won't be the one that crushes him. It's better that he doesn't know. It's better he never knows.

This really freaking sucks.

22

THE KNOCK AT THE FRONT DOOR IS LIKE A DEATH KNELL. I REALLY wish Kris and Dani weren't coming for dinner. My brain just isn't in the right place. I keep seeing Zack's face, hear his words echoing in my ears.

My mom opens the door, jarring my thoughts. She greets Kris with a hug. Dani walks in after her and heads for the other couch, not even acknowledging me. She can't still be feeling the effects from getting wasted the other night. This is most likely more drama.

Kris follows behind, and the room fills with this tense energy that makes me shift in my seat. Probably because none of us are feeling really friendly lately. Kris and Mom chat back and forth, but I'm not really paying attention. I zone out, allowing phrases from Zack's video to keep looping through my brain. Guilt settles in too. Shouldn't I tell someone about what I saw? His parents have to know, but why doesn't anyone else?

"How's school, Tori?" Kris asks, dragging me from my own morose thoughts.

I try to read the room. But nothing has changed since they first walked in, except Dani is giving me an odd look. "Uh, fine."

"Dani tells me that you're working with Nick on a school project, and that you two are getting pretty close." That's what Kris says, but what I really hear is, *So you're the whore who's stealing my daughter's man right out from under her—how dare you.*

"For crying out loud," I say under my breath. I can't take this right now. "I don't need this today."

Kris sits up taller. "What was that?"

"We're partners on a project. I don't want him. I don't want to date anyone right now."

She nods her approval. "Well, you shouldn't be dating anyone right now with how unstable you obviously still are."

Dani sucks in a harsh breath and I sit there like I just got slapped across the face. I've had enough of this for tonight and it's been all of five minutes. I really want to call Kris all sorts of nasty names, but that'll just make things worse.

"What did you just say to my daughter?" I hear my mom ask in a quiet deadly voice.

Kris wipes a piece of lint off her pants, acting like this conversation is fine. "Don't pretend you don't agree with me. We talked about this the other day."

And with that, I'm out. I turn and head up the stairs, ignoring my mom calling my name. What is wrong with these people? Do they think it's okay to talk like that while I'm in the room? Forget applauding her for standing up for me, because who knows what else her and Kris are talking about. I storm into my room and slam the door. The raised voices from downstairs still reach me. I flop down onto my bed and throw my arm over my face. Stress gnaws at my stomach. Can this day get any worse?

I hear footsteps outside my room and I bring my arm down. Why did I just jinx myself? The door opens and I look up. Dani stands near the foot of my bed.

"I can't do this right now, Dani. Please just leave me alone."

Her eyes dart around the room, looking anywhere but at me. "I just wanted to tell you that I think my mom was way out of line."

I sit up so she'll focus on me. "Thanks, but I can't keep telling you that I don't want anything to do with Nick in that way. I don't know what to do to make you believe me. I'm sorry I have to work on this project with him. I tried to get out of that class, but there was nothing else open. What do you want from me?" I'm at the end of my rope.

"He just seems to really like you," she says.

It's like she doesn't listen to me when I talk to her. I can't control his feelings and she knows mine. "We're friends. But I can't read his mind. And you gotta stop punishing me for something I can't control."

I get up and walk past her to the door. "I need to use the bathroom."

I walk into the bathroom and sit on the lip of the tub rubbing my temples. Maybe if I hide in here long enough, she'll be gone when I come back.

I give it about five minutes and then walk back into my room. Dani's sitting on my bed as I enter but stands up right away, shoving her hands into the front of her sweatshirt. We stare at each other for a few moments. And I try to remember the girl who was one of my best friends when I was little. Because that picture is fading the longer I live here.

She rocks back on her heels. "I'll see you tomorrow morning?"

"Sure," I tell her. I'm probably going to need to find a new way to school. Maybe I should finally get my driver's license.

She walks out of the room, leaving me by myself. I lie on the bed and listen to the front door open and close.

My phone pings from my pocket. Nick's name flashes on my screen. I huff out a breath. But I still smile in spite of myself. This guy. He always has great timing in taking my mind off things. But as quickly as I smile, it falls.

Nick — I bet you wanna go race go-karts again

A tear skims down my cheek. I can't tell him. I can't be the one to ruin his life. I take a deep breath in and fall into the text messages. Desperately putting a wall up in my mind.

Me — I was pretty amazing

Nick — let's not get ahead of ourselves. You couldn't even touch the awesomeness of my driving skills.

My face splits into a smile. Cocky jerk.

Nick — are you coming over tomorrow?

Huh? Tomorrow? Did we talk about hanging out?

Nick — to work on the project

I want to smack myself in the forehead. I flop back on my bed, letting the phone fall to my chest. Where did I think he was going with that text? I bring my phone back in front of my face.

Me — don't you have practice?

Nick — yeah but we can do it after. Just come over to the garage

Me — k

Nick — see you tomorrow speed racer

I laugh out loud. Dork. Who would have thought that this guy would make me smile? Someone knocks on my door and I drop my phone to my lap.

"Can I come in?" my mom asks from the other side.

The smile still on my face immediately falls. "Yeah," I say.

She opens the door and peeks her head in, scanning the room before her eyes land on me. What's she looking for? Another broken mirror? They haven't let me have one since after the last incident.

She squeezes in and closes the door, leaning against it. "I'm sorry about Kris," she says.

"You shouldn't be apologizing for her," I tell Mom. Now, she *should* apologize for telling Kris things that I don't want her knowing.

She looks down at her feet, her hands fidgeting with the bottom of her shirt.

"I know, but..." She draws a deep breath. "I shouldn't tell her so much."

Wow. She finally lifts her face to mine.

"How hard was it to admit being wrong?" I ask, starting to giggle.

"Victoria," she says with the right amount of indignation. But she laughs a little. "You have no idea." Her eyes seem a little more alive. "I'll limit what I tell her about you. And nothing you wouldn't want her to know."

"I would appreciate that. Don't know how you're friends with that woman."

She gives a halfhearted shrug. "I've known Kris since the third grade."

"So?" I ask, because honestly, when a friend sucks like that, why keep them?

She glances back down. "She hasn't always been this..." she trails off.

"Bitter?"

Her eyes narrow on me. But come on—Kris is super bitter.

"I was going to say testy," she says.

"Uh-huh."

"Does Dani ever talk about her parents' divorce?" she asks.

I shake my head. "We've never talked about it."

"It was really bad. Her ex-husband said some things that can't be unsaid."

"Like what?" I ask.

"If I start telling you all that, then I'm no better than Kris was earlier. And I'm trying to be better at keeping my confidences. But it wasn't good. She hasn't bounced back yet."

"She can't use that for an excuse forever," I say. Don't see me running around looking for sympathy and treating people like garbage.

She sighs. "No, but everyone heals at their own pace."

Don't I know it—and it feels like my mom is talking more about me than Kris with that tidbit.

As if she senses the tension mounting in the room, she turns toward the door. "Okay, well that's all I wanted to talk to you about." She waits at the door, looking at me. I'm not sure what she wants. Is she wanting me to talk about my own healing? I'm not ready for that.

"There's some food in the fridge if you want it."

"Thanks. I think I'm just gonna crash."

Her hand tightens on the door frame, but she quickly releases it. "All right. Night, baby. Love you." She pulls the door shut.

"Love you too," I whisper at the closed door.

23

"Hey, speed racer," Nick says as he steps next to my locker.

"Speed racer?" Dani asks, looking between us.

Nick's face lights up and he points at me. "You should see her drive a go-kart."

I want to shove my face in my locker, but instead I turn and look at Dani. Her face is scrunched up. "Go-karts?" she asks me, but Nick answers.

"Yeah, we went on Saturday."

I want to smack him—like take my Algebra book and smash it into his arm. Wait, he needs that arm for basketball. Stomach then, definitely stomach.

"It was research," I say, but I'm grasping at straws to appease her and I can tell she knows it by that narrowed eye look I'm getting.

She moves her hands to her hips. "Research?"

"Why are you repeating everything we say like a parrot?" Nick asks.

I rub my forehead. For crying out loud. What is wrong with him? He just needs to shut up.

She folds her arms tight across her chest. "It sounds like a date," she says, her voice heavy with accusation.

I wave my hands in the air. "Definitely not a date."

"Kinda," Nick says at the same time.

"What the hell, Tori?!" Dani shouts.

Nick's jaw drops a little and people turn their heads toward us to see the drama unfold.

"He's just kidding. Besides, he knows that I don't like him like that, at all," I tell her, desperately trying to reassure her.

"Hey," Nick says, completely offended.

"You're not helping," I say through gritted teeth. I seriously might murder him at this point.

"Why didn't you tell me?" she asks, sounding betrayed.

I run a hand through my hair. "Last night wasn't the best night," I remind her. The last thing on my mind was telling her about going go-karting with Nick.

The warning bell rings.

"We're not done talking about this," she says and turns and storms away.

Why do I feel like I totally just got scolded?

"You coming to homeroom?" Nick asks.

I chuck some books into the locker. "You going to cause any more problems for me?" I ask.

"What did I do?"

"You are so freaking dense." I slam my locker closed. If he didn't seem so genuinely clueless about how much of an idiot he's being, I'd shove him in my locker too. "Let's go," I tell him.

We head down the hall. "It *was* kind of a date," he says in a low voice.

"Nick!"

I see his small smirk out of the corner of my eye. That does it —I'm definitely going to murder him. I could totally handle jail.

We reach the door and I shove him out of the way. His laughter follows me into the room.

"What's so funny?" Regina asks as I reach my seat next to her.

I shake my head. "Nothing, he's just an idiot," I tell her.

She nods in complete understanding. "Definitely," she says.

* * *

"Saw you at my house on Friday," Rossi says as soon as I reach my seat in auto. He's way closer to me than I want. I can feel his nasty breath on my neck, and it causes my body to lock. "Kept wishing you'd take that hoodie off so I could see what's underneath."

"You need to back off, man," Nick says, as he walks up to our table.

Rossi lifts his hands in the air. "We're just talking."

He is so vile.

Nick leans into him, making his point clear. "You can see she doesn't like it, so walk away."

My eyes dart between the two of them. Nick's hands are clenched tight into fists. Whoa, I've never seen him this pissed.

But Rossi doesn't back down. "Last thing I heard you two aren't together, so maybe you should run along," Rossi says, his face set into a haughty expression.

I choke down the bile in my throat. Enough.

"Stop." My voice comes out weak and that pisses me off. They both look at me in shock. I take a deep breath and force myself to look Rossi in the eye. "You need to leave me alone. I don't like you. You gross me out. Find someone else to bother, because I'm done."

I turn around and look blankly at the papers on my desk. My heart is a freaking jackhammer and I have to keep swallowing the building saliva in my mouth.

"Not worth the trouble," I hear Rossi say.

Nick pulls out the chair next to me. I feel his eyes focused on my face. "What?" I ask without looking at him.

He doesn't answer right away so I turn my head toward him. He's got a huge cheesy smile on his face. "I'm just so proud of you for telling him off," he says.

"Shut up," I tell him, but my face goes hot.

He bursts into loud laughter, and all the guys in the room turn toward us. How could they not? Nick's laugh is deep and contagious. Hearing it makes even me smile a little. But my smile drops. As I watch his whole face light up, an image of Zack's face flashes in my mind. If I tell him about the video, he's not going to laugh like that again.

"You still coming over tonight?" he asks, a smile still spread across his face.

His question pulls me out of my thoughts, and I nod. "Well, unless you want to do all the work on the car yourself, which I'm totally okay with, by the way."

"I'll see you at seven, then."

* * *

"Why is Dani sitting over there with Gretchen?" Regina asks when she sits next to me.

I look down at the table. "I'm surprised she didn't text you," I say.

She checks her phone. "Huh. Nothing," she says. "What happened?"

I turn my head just enough to catch a glimpse of Dani. She's waving her hands in the air and her mouth is moving quickly. Gretchen leans in, slack-jawed.

Might as well get this out of the way now. "She's mad at me."

"Because of Nick?" she asks.

Someone sits down in front of us. I look up and see Britney.

135

"Who's mad?" Britney asks.

"Dani," Regina answers.

I run my hands through my hair. "Nick and I drove go-karts on Saturday night," I tell them.

"Oooh," Regina says. "Like a date?"

"No. I tried telling her it wasn't anything. But Nick is a big idiot and said it was kind of a date," I tell them.

Britney looks down at her fries and starts laughing. "What?" I ask. I see nothing funny about this whole situation.

"You must see it," Britney says.

"Oh, I totally do," Regina adds in.

I look between the two of them as they share a knowing look. "Yeah, I'm still lost," I say.

"Everyone can see there's something there with you and Nick, and that pisses Dani off," Britney says.

"You may not want to agree with it, but Regina is not wrong," Britney adds in.

I push my lunch away, no longer hungry. "Dani likes him, why doesn't he pursue that?" I ask. And I want them to answer because I don't have one.

"You can't help who you like or who you don't like," Regina tells me in a gentle voice.

I put my head down on the table. I can't be what Nick wants or needs. I can barely be friends with him. Dani is practically in love with him and yet he doesn't see it.

Regina pats me on the shoulder. "It can't be that bad having Nick like you," she says.

"Except for the fact that one of her friends loves him and is pissed at her," Britney says.

Without lifting my head, I point a finger at Britney, she's so freaking accurate.

Regina chuckles. "Well, I guess you're kinda screwed then," she says.

24

THE GARAGE DOOR IS CLOSED AS I WALK UP THE DRIVEWAY. HE always has the garage open when I come over. I look to the front door. Should I go knock? What if his parents are home? Why am I getting so worked up about this? The cold wind pushes its way through my hoodie and makes the decision for me. I trudge up the stairs like I'm approaching the gates of Hell.

My finger hovers over the doorbell, but before I can press it the door whips open. I stumble back and grab the railing before I fall down the stairs.

"Tori?" a very smiley woman asks me. Her green eyes dance in excitement. And she seriously bounces on her toes. No wonder Nick is such a happy guy. His mom is like Christmas in the form of a human body.

"Uh, yeah, that's me," I tell her.

"I'm Cindy, Nick's mom. Come in, come in," she says and then stands to the side.

I walk in the front door and scan the space for Nick. He's nowhere to be seen. "Is Nick home?"

137

"Oh yes, just taking a shower. All sweaty from basketball. Have a seat on the couch," she says.

I make my way over to the couch and spot the pictures on the walls. There are so many. Nick stands next to three other guys, all sort of carbon copies of each other. I can't even imagine being in a room with all of them.

"Nick's my youngest of four," she says, her eyes looking at the photo I was staring at a moment ago.

"Oh," I say, sitting on the couch while she sits in a chair across from me. I shift under her chipper gaze. I kind of assumed she'd leave me alone while I waited for Nick.

"You live in Zack's house?" Cindy asks.

"Yeah," I tell her. "Do you know why they moved?"

Her smile falters a little.

"It's just—it seems like it was out of the blue. Everyone says they left without telling anyone," I say quickly.

She looks toward the stairs. I can still hear the water from the shower. "Well, we know about Zack going to the wilderness school. But it was a surprise when his parents left. His mom, Denise, sent me an e-mail saying the family needed a change."

I raise my eyebrows. Yeah, they definitely needed a change. I can't believe they just left and said nothing.

"But didn't Zack like disappear in the middle of the night?" I ask. I bite my lip. I've got to stop asking questions; I don't know who knows what. And she's probably wondering why I'm fishing.

She tilts her head to the side, her eyes unfocused. "I just assumed that's how the program worked. Actually, I'm not really sure," she says.

"Oh."

The shower shuts off. Thank goodness.

"Mom, is Tori here yet?" Nick yells from the upstairs.

"Yup, she's sitting down here with me. I was about to pull out the pictures from when you were potty trained," she calls up to him.

Complete silence from above.

"I'm kidding. Hurry up and get dressed...before I pull them out," she says.

Fast footfalls sound above us.

"He'll be down probably within sixty seconds," she assures me with a wink.

I grin. It's fun having Nick be the one flustered for a change.

"So, what made you guys move here all the way from Arizona?" she asks.

"Uh..." It's a simple question, and I have an answer for it. But for some reason, it feels wrong to give that to her.

Feet pound down the stairs, saving me from having to tell her anything. "Sorry I took so long," Nick says, out of breath.

I spring from the couch. "It's fine. Ready to get working?" If we stay any longer, his mom is going to want me to answer that question.

"Yeah, let's go," he says.

"It was nice to meet you, Tori," Cindy says.

"You too, Mrs. Janus," I tell her and hurry after Nick.

We walk down the hall and then out a door into what feels like a walk-in freezer. The air freezes in my lungs and I immediately wrap my arms tight around my middle. "It's like the arctic in here," I say, my cloudy puffs of breath only emphasizing my point more.

"Yeah, sorry about that. I forgot to get the space heater on earlier to warm the place up. Come sit over here and I'll turn it up," he says.

We walk over to the pile of car parts we've been working on. Thank goodness the stool is wood and not metal. Nick fiddles with the space heater. With his attention elsewhere, I slide my cuffs off and into my pocket. It was too awkward working with them and gloves last time.

The cold seeps into my fingers and sharp stabbing pins spread across them. I shove them in between my knees, desperately trying to warm them.

"Here's some gloves." Nick turns back toward me, and his eyes look down to my hands sandwiched between my legs.

"Rubbing them would be better," he says and then makes to grab for my hands.

I pull them up to stop him or get away, I'm not sure. But it doesn't matter. He takes a sharp breath—it's too late. I know what he sees. How can he not? They're jagged and dark pink. It might have been almost a year ago, but these scars aren't fading anytime soon.

I put my hands in my lap and shift my eyes to the side. I can't look at his eyes. I can't.

"Tell me about them?" he whispers. The feel of his fingers against my hand barely registers as he grazes them. But it's enough that I felt it.

I snap my eyes back to him. "Obviously you can tell what they're from." Why am I getting so angry?

"Tell me?" he asks again.

I jerk my arm away from his touch, and he lets me.

My hands tangle in my hair.

My breath comes faster.

My heart pounds.

Do it, I chant to myself. *Do it. Tell someone.*

I look up and find his eyes watching me. No judgement. No sympathy. Just patience.

Do it.

"I tried to kill myself." Such a short sentence, but such a heart-wrenching one.

His mouth opens and closes a few times. I know he wants to say something, but whatever it is, I'm not ready to hear it, so I raise my hand. "Don't ask why. Just don't, please?"

His lips press together tightly, and he nods.

Words start spewing forth, words that have been locked up for way too long. "My mom found me. I was already unconscious. That's why we moved here. They thought this place would fix me."

"All those quotes on the wall?"

A sad laugh escapes. "Yeah." I run a shaky hand through my hair. "My mom's hoping they'll all seep into my brain without me knowing it."

He looks at my wrists, now lying limp in my lap. "Do you want to...you know, try that again?" he asks, gesturing to them.

"No."

He looks me in the eye, and I have to force myself not to flinch. "No? Are you sure?"

Am I? Some days I don't know how I make it through, but I make it nonetheless. I conquered yesterday. Hell, I conquered *that* day, after all.

Yes.

"Yes, I'm sure."

"Good."

I rear back. "Good? That's it? No twenty questions about it?" I was expecting a long list, too. At the very least, the one question on why I did it.

He gives me a tender smile. "You'll tell me if or when you want to. I'm just happy you're here now."

Who is this guy? And where was he last year?

* * *

"I actually told him about the reason why my parents moved us out here."

Dr. West's chair creaks as she leans back. "So, he knows you tried committing suicide." It's not a question.

I twist the cuff around my left wrist as I nod.

"And how do you feel now that Nick knows?"

Isn't that a loaded question? I pull on my cuff again. "Exposed. Like everything wrong with me is on display for him to see." I blow out a breath. "I'm not sure. He didn't freak out, so that's a positive, right?"

"How *did* he take it?" she asks with a little hesitation.

"I think it surprised him. He wanted to know if I was going to try it again. I think that freaked him out. It was hard to really read him, though, because my brain was all over the place."

"Do you regret telling him?"

I stare at her desk. Do I? Sometimes the tightness in my chest says yes. But then, something rises in me, soothing those knots. Nodding to myself, I come to a decision.

"You know what? Oddly enough, no, I don't."

"It's good you've found a good friend to tell."

"Friend?" I nearly choke on the word.

"Well, what else would you call Nick?"

"Uh…" Wait. Is she— "Are you…laughing at me?"

She waves a hand in front of her face as she tries to calm herself down. "Sorry, totally unprofessional, but you look so shocked that I suggested Nick is a good friend."

I drop my head back against the chair and cover my face with my arm. "I've become so pathetic that my therapist laughs at me." But I laugh with her, and it feels great.

25

———

"Hey, where were you this morning?" I ask Dani as I stop next to her locker.

Her face snaps toward me and I take a step back. Her mouth pinches and her nostrils flare. "You expected me to pick you up?" Every word drips with anger and disgust.

Whoa. What am I missing? "Uh, yeah. You said you were going to."

"Everything is not about you." Her voice is harsh and ugly.

"Dani, what's the deal?" I whisper my question. We're already starting to attract attention.

"What's the deal?!" So much for not attracting more attention. "You...you selfish whore. You had to move here. You had to ruin things."

"Did she really just call me a whore?" I ask myself under by breath. I'm honestly confused by this and why my mind latched on to that one tidbit, I'm not even sure. But Dani's on a roll and she's not going to stop.

"You know I like him, but that doesn't matter to you."

"What are you talking about?"

"And now he wants to take *you* to prom." Okay, now I'm slightly offended that the idea of someone taking me to prom disgusts her.

"Nick?" I ask.

"Who else?"

I close my eyes, preparing myself for the same speech we've had a dozen times. "There's nothing going on. I'm not interested in dating him, or anyone. I don't know what else I can say to make you see that."

"Bull. He told me he wants to ask you."

My shoulders slump and I release a slow breath. "I don't want to go to prom with anyone. What do you want me to do? I can't control his feelings."

Apparently, that was the wrong thing to say.

Dani slams her locker door, and the whole hall freezes. "Why don't you slit your wrists again and finish what you started." She storms away, leaving me exposed to everyone.

The silence in the hall is deadly.

The stares are weighted and pressing down on me.

My heart bangs painfully in my chest. I'm going to be sick.

I look down at my feet. *Move*, I command them, but they stay planted.

My breath gets choppy and my vision wavers.

"Tori?" Nick's voice floats to me, breaking the silence in the hall.

I meet his eyes. Eyes that ask if I'm okay. His hands move, reaching toward me, probably to comfort. And that's what finally makes my feet move away from my locker. I can't bear to see the pity that will soon fill his eyes.

Words drift in my ears as I walk to homeroom.

"...transfered..."

"...so sad..."

"...cuffs..."

Part of me screams to hold my head high, telling me to ignore them. I'm alive. But there's a bigger part that whispers the *shame* over and over again.

I take one step.

"She tried to kill herself?"

My brittle heart starts falling apart piece by piece. Another step.

"Probably wanted attention..."

My throat tightens. Almost there.

"...tried to steal Nick..."

For the love of all that's holy!

A hand wraps around my arm, snapping me out of my own free fall. I wrench it free and turn, ready to unleash hell on whoever touched me.

My hand freezes midair. Nick.

"Are you okay?" he asks as he pushes my frozen hand down. And I let him.

I feel so many eyes on me, watching the two of us. "When did my life turn into a bad teen movie?"

A small smile forms on his lips, but it drops as someone walks by whispering about my suicide attempt. He moves closer to me, probably afraid I might finally snap. Smart man. "She had no right." He says it so vehemently.

I take deep breaths to stop the onslaught of tears that are finally trying to break through. "You want to skip school today?" he asks.

"That's going to make people talk."

"They're going to talk anyways; might as well not be around to listen to it. Besides, it's Friday. Something's sure to happen this weekend that'll make them forget all about this by Monday."

I look at his hopeful face.

"So sad," someone whispers as they pass by me.

That does it. I can't take this for a full day. "Yeah. Let's go."

We turn and walk to the nearest exit. The whole way, people stare and whisper to each other. They probably think Dani is right me and Nick, but I can't care about that right now. All I care about is walking through the metal door ahead of us and the promise of air.

* * *

"So, a lifeguard chair?" I ask.

Our feet dangle over the edge. Steam curls toward our faces from our hot chocolate. It's freezing out and yet here we are at the beach, sipping hot drinks.

"I usually come here on summer nights; not so much in the winter," he says, eyes focused ahead.

I nod, looking out to the water. The sand is littered with frozen sea foam, so I doubt anyone else will be intruding on us. It's a pretty isolated beach.

After a moment, Nick breaks our comfortable silence. "Want to talk about it?" he asks.

"Not really."

"Okay." He doesn't sound disappointed. If anything, his voice tells me that this conversation is in my court.

I look back at the lone beach. "Why here?" I ask him.

He leans his head back, letting the sun shine on his face for a minute. "Zack and I've been coming here since we were kids. At first just to play in the water, and later, to get away from his parents. They were always fighting."

My stomach pulses with pain at the mention of Zack. I can't keep putting off telling him what I know. But right now, Nick is the only person talking to me. I don't want him to look at me like everyone else is right now. I can't handle any more loss. I don't want to lose him.

Whoa. I look at his smiling face. The realization that I don't want to lose him almost makes me fall off our high perch.

"Of course, we would bring girls here, too. It's an impressive spot, after all." He keeps reminiscing, not having any clue that I'm having an epiphany mixed with a panic attack.

* * *

"Do I have to tell him?" I ask.

"Well, you could live with the guilt of keeping that secret, slowly eating away at you. Sounds like a lovely life, right?" Dr. West asks, but it's not really a question.

That guilt is already eating away at me. Knowing that Zack killed himself, having that knowledge, is not something I'd wish on my worst enemy. I have the power to answer a lot of questions, but ruin a lot of lives.

"It feels like there are things you aren't telling me," she says, confirming my suspicions that she knows I'm holding a lot more back. That I actually found a lot more than just Zack's art.

"Sorry?"

She tilts her head and gives me a patronizing look. "I wouldn't be good at my job if I didn't ask. But you can tell me when you're ready."

"How do you know I'll ever be ready?" In truth that is a question for her, but for me as well. I'm not sure I ever want to tell anyone.

"You coming to see me gives me the answer that you will. But back to your friend. The longer you wait, the worse it will be when he finds out. And make no mistake, he will. Things like this have a way of coming to the surface, especially the things we want to hide the most."

I hate when she's right.

I slump further down in my chair. "How do I even go about telling him?"

She raises an eyebrow at me. I know that look; it means her answer is going to piss me off. "I'm not going to tell you."

I throw my hands in the air. "Seriously? Isn't that what you're here for?"

"How can you begin to heal if I give you the answers to every problem you face? I can give you the tools, but you need to put in the work."

She sounds like one of my mom's motivational posters.

"Don't look at me like that," she admonishes me. "I know it sounds cheesy, but if you actually turn my words around in your head, you'll know it's sound advice."

I cover my face, blocking her out. Blocking everything out. "I'm going to lose him," I whisper.

"You might, but that's not your decision. Respect Nick enough to let him decide how to react."

26

I rip open my nightstand and shove everything aside looking for that single scrap of paper with the link to Zack's video. I empty the whole drawer, but it's not there. Maybe it's under the bed? It's got to be. I can't lose this. I erased the history on my computer already, afraid my mom would see it and freak out.

I drop down to my knees and check under the bed. Not there. Damn it. I ransack my own room, shoving things around in my dresser, pulling shoes out of the closet; I'm two seconds away from flipping my bed.

"What are you doing?" my mom asks from my bedroom door. I didn't even hear her open it.

I run my hands through my hair. "Have you seen a slip of paper with a website on it? I can't find it."

"No, I haven't been in your room since the other night when Kris and Dani were here."

My eyes keep scanning the room. Where is it? My heart is hammering in my chest and I'm literally moments away from puking. "Was it important?" she asks.

Only important enough to destroy a ton of people's lives. But I can't tell her that. "Yeah, I need it for school." The lie falls easily from my lips.

"Well, why don't we check downstairs," she suggests.

Why didn't I think of that? I rush past her and race downstairs. It should be here. I didn't take it out of the house. I wouldn't. Someone could find it and I don't want to deal with the fallout from that.

We search under couch cushions, the junk drawer, which hasn't really had the chance to become a junk drawer yet. My mom even checks her room. It's gone. My hands tremble as I realize that I lost it, and the monumental problem now lying on my shoulders. Where could it be? Could someone have it? If anyone finds it and they trace it back to me...Nick will never forgive me. Britney will look at me with disgust. I don't know what to do. Tears stream down my face.

My mom rubs my arm. "Don't worry, we'll just tell your teacher. I'm sure it'll be okay." She does her best to comfort me, but it's not helping.

I'm not sure what will. This changes everything; I want to curl up in a ball on the floor.

Then a thought occurs to me. Could it be up in the attic? I doubt it, but at this point, who knows. I haven't checked there.

"I'm going to my room," I tell her and make my way up the stairs.

Every step feels like I'm trudging through sand. Like my mind knows that problems are coming and they're just weighing me down. I close my door and make my way to the closet. Why am I even bothering looking? I haven't been up there since I found it. Instead, I slide down the closet wall and collapse on the floor. There's no way a slip of paper got legs and made its way up to the attic. Maybe I should just forget about it. Maybe if I don't tell anyone about losing it, it'll never surface. Or maybe it'll magically appear back on my nightstand.

I keep telling myself that over and over again. It's the only way that I can make it without breaking down. But there's this voice in the back of my mind that's screaming at me that I'm screwed.

* * *

Something isn't right. I knew school would be rough today after what happened with Dani in the hall last Friday, but this is something else. Homeroom just feels wrong. I look around trying to pinpoint what it is, and then Dani's eyes lock with mine. She shouldn't be here. Her lips pull into an ugly smile, but she quickly schools her features and nudges Nick's arm. He slowly turns in his chair. And when he faces me, my stomach plummets at his expression. He looks destroyed.

"Tori, good. You're here. I was just showing Nick what I found in your room," Dani says with a sneer.

I inch toward the computer they're surrounding and see the piece of paper that's supposed to be on my nightstand. Time stops, and I know that *sounds* cliché, but it feels like the whole room is holding its breath as I slowly raise my eyes to the screen.

It's Zack's video.

"Now, I'm just wondering why you kept this a secret from us. Especially since we're supposed to be your *friends*." She says friends like it's a curse.

Nothing comes out of my mouth. Why didn't she talk to me about the paper? Why is she doing this? Does she not get what she's done?

Dani looks back down at Nick and rubs a hand across his shoulder. She can't be for real. This is all over Nick, and her feelings for him.

"Tori?" The sound of Nick's broken voice shreds whatever resolve I had left. It makes me want to run and hide.

I can't look him in the eye. I can't deal with the anguish that's probably filling them. I stare at the floor trying to think of how to answer him.

He slams his fists on the table, his body shaking with anger. "Say something!"

I cower away from him. This is not the Nick I've come to know.

"Say something," he pleads in a painful whisper.

But what can I say? I can't.

I grab my bag and run from homeroom. I sprint down the hall, hearing Nick scream my name. The exit is ahead, and I burst through the doors into the blinding sun. My feet hit the stairs, and I keep running.

I have to get away.

I hit the parking lot and race away from the school. I can't go to the house—Mom's there and she'll ask too many questions. I head toward the water instead. No one will be there.

I finally reach a small beach with a lifeguard chair, and I scramble up into it.

And I break. Huge sobs rack my body. The betrayal on Nick's face is at the front of my mind.

This is why I was so afraid to tell him. I knew it would devastate him. And deep down, I knew it would ruin whatever we were building. He'll never be able to look at me the same. And every time he sees me, he's going to see Zack. I wonder if he wishes it was me that was gone instead of his best friend. Why am I still here and Zack's not?

I thought maybe I was getting better, but that was a lie. I rip the cuffs off my wrists and stare at my ugly scars. Even hidden, they define me, and I'm so tired. I'm tired of the constant sadness threatening to engulf me. I'm tired of the forced smiles and the standard answer of "I'm fine." This isn't living. This is barely breathing. How much longer until the precarious ledge I'm clinging to crumbles?

I pull out my phone and ignore all the texts flooding it. I find Dr. West's number and send her a simple but gut-wrenching text. *I'm ready.*

27

———

"What are you ready for, Tori?" Dr. West asks in the gentlest voice I've ever heard her use.

It took me thirty minutes to walk here. And all that time I knew she'd ask this question. But I don't even know how to begin to answer it. Living this way is so exhausting. Something has to give. The skin under my cuffs burns, and I can't stop rubbing at them.

"I can't—" My voice wavers, and I clear my throat. "I can't live like this anymore."

"And how are you living?"

My knee won't stop bouncing and the urge to throw up keeps increasing. "Some days, it's like I poison everything I touch. Some days I think if I wasn't here, life would be so much easier for everyone else. Some nights I go to bed just mentally spent and I wake up with the weight of living that feels like it's crushing me. You know, I thought this would be gone. And it'll go away for a bit, but then it's back.

"I know that being bitter and angry wears on your soul. But then, letting people in and letting yourself feel everything? It's almost worse. I can't work out which way is better, but something has to give. Because my heart just wants to give up when it gets tough."

She stares at me with kind eyes. This is the most I've ever opened up to her. She gives me time, not forcing me to go fast, but encouraging me.

"Why did you try to commit suicide?"

I shake my head. No one knows this.

She gets up and walks over to the chair next to mine. "Tori, if you want to change how you live, you have to face the past, or it'll keep hampering your future."

Tears stream down my cheeks, crashing onto my clasped hands. "I've never told anyone before." My voice sounds so weak... so much like it did that night.

"Don't you think it's time?" she asks, and I swear it almost sounds like a plea.

I swallow the thick ball of emotion in my throat and the stream of tears increases. A sound escapes me, and man does it reflect the pain lodged in my heart and soul. "This guy I was dating—" A sob erupts.

She reaches out and clasps her hand with mine. "You can do this. It's just you and me here, Tori. No one else. Take back whatever was taken from you."

I clear my throat. "I was dating this guy, John. We'd been together for a couple of months when my grandma died."

The thought of losing her cracks open my heart even wider, and I take a stuttering breath.

"I didn't take her death well," I tell her.

She gives my hand a squeeze. "That's understandable."

"John had been pushing me a lot lately; he wanted to be more..." I trail off trying to say the word.

"Physical?" she offers.

"Yeah, physical. I kept telling him that I wasn't ready, and he kept bringing up his ex-girlfriend and how they had slept together. The night after the funeral he came and picked me up."

Flashes from that night go off before my eyes. My body shudders. *"Come on Tori, I'm tired of waiting. Jen loved it."*

"Tori. Tori, come back to me. He can't get you here." Dr. West's voice centers me.

I stare at the painting over her shoulder, but I don't see it. I see the dark parking lot, the shadows that surrounded the car when he turned it off. The time on the clock: 9:27. The trees that seemed to encroach on us. "He took me to a park. He said he wanted to talk in the back seat."

"I'm not ready yet," I whisper as he reaches for my shirt.

He grips it harder in his hands and I hear it tear a little. "Fine, then just let me kiss you and hold you."

"His hands were everywhere and when I told him it was too much..." I can't stop the heart-wrenching sounds that come out of my mouth.

His hands on my skin feel so wrong. He's too strong for me.

My body flinches at the mere memory of his hands acting like they owned me.

"I told him no!" I scream.

I look at Dr. West through blurry eyes. "I told him no," I say again, with all the feeling in my tattered soul.

Her arms encircle me. And the feel of her tears on my hair pierces a piece of my heart that I thought was gone.

"He acted like what he did was no big deal," I say through sobs. "A few days later he sent me a bunch of texts saying he was back with Jen. I couldn't"—I shake my head, "I didn't want to live anymore after that. I felt...I *still* feel so dirty. It felt so wrong. He took what he wanted and threw me away."

I try to clear the emotion strangling my throat, but it does no good. "I took a knife from the kitchen drawer and sat on the floor in the bathroom for a while. Every breath felt like his hands were around my throat. My mind felt so out of control. I kept spinning down into this hell and it was too much. I just wanted it to stop. So I dragged the knife up and across my wrists. And then my mom found me."

She hugs me for a minute longer.

"I'm so proud of you for telling me that."

I pull back and look into her eyes. A huge part of me feels laid bare before her. But there's this tiny little part that feels like it clicked back into place. And with that is the fear that it'll slip away again. That I won't be able to keep hold of that piece.

"When will it not affect me so much?" I ask in desperation.

"It will always affect you. But *you* get to decide how much and in what way. This is your life, Tori, and you have something, that no one else does, to add to this world whether small or big. Don't let John take that from you. Don't let him take from us what we get from you."

I nod, knowing it'll take time to believe her words more.

"What made you finally come see me?"

Nick's angry screams ring through my ears.

"Do you remember how I told you about Zack?"

She nods. "The boy with all the art that lived in your house before you?"

"Yeah. What I didn't tell you was that I found a video." I push through the guilt plaguing me. "It was his suicide note."

She raises a brow.

"No one knows he committed suicide," I tell her softly.

She lets out a whoosh of air. "When did you find out?"

"About a week ago. There was a little slip of paper with a website written on it." I try taking some deep breaths, because it feels like she's going to judge me on this, and I don't know why. "It was his suicide note. But it was for a specific person."

She waits patiently. Not pushing.

"It was for Nick."

"Did you show the video to him?" she asks.

I hang my head. "No. When I first found the room, I was still kind of uncomfortable around him and I didn't know what to do. The more time passed, the better I came to know him, and the harder it became to tell him. I saw how my parents changed when they learned what I'd done. And after I found the video, I knew I didn't want Nick to become like that."

She steeples her fingers. "I'm guessing he found out."

That's an understatement. "My friend—well I guess she's not my friend anymore—showed him today at school. She must have found the slip of paper in my room."

She stares at me for a long time. "What happened next?"

Stupid tears start pouring down my face again. I didn't know I had any left. "He was so mad and hurt. He kept asking why."

"And why didn't you tell him?"

"Because I was afraid I would lose him and it would change him." It's true, I don't want to see his eyes turn ugly and his personality bleed away.

After a long pause, Dr. West gently asks, "So, what are you going to do now? And what about this friend that showed him?"

"I don't know," I whisper.

I don't think I can ever be friends with Dani again. The nasty look of triumph on her face was enough to convince me that I don't really know her anymore. And how could I ever trust her?

"Tell me everything you found in that room."

And I do. I tell her about the notes that Zack left for Nick to hand out, the drawings, everything.

When I'm finally done talking, Dr. West writes something in her notebook and then looks up at me with a determined face. "All right, I want you to stay home the next few days. You went through a lot of emotions today. Just lay low until Wednesday, and then on Monday we'll have you come in. If you need me before that, just text me. And Tori..."

I look up and meet her eyes.

"Thank you for entrusting me with what happened to you last year. I know that was hard for you."

I give her a tight-lipped smile and I leave her office feeling the strongest pulse of light for the first time in a year. What started as a small flicker of hope is steadily growing.

Until my phone rings.

28

"Victoria Adams! Why are you not at school?" my mom screeches through the phone.

I pull it away from my ear as she continues yelling about calling hospitals and the police station.

"Mom!" I finally yell back into the phone.

"Well, what do you have to say for yourself?" she demands.

"I was at Dr. West's office."

And just like that, all the anger is out of her voice. "Really?" she asks, her voice filled with suppressed hope.

"Yeah, Mom," I tell her.

I hear her sniffle into the phone. "Oh sweetie, that's so good."

Only my mom would be proud of me for skipping school and going to see my therapist on my own. "I'm just leaving now, so I'm coming home. Sorry I worried you."

"That's okay, just let me know the next time you decide to run out of school in the middle of the day." The way she says that you would think it was a common occurrence for me.

"K, can you ask Dad to come get me?" I ask.

"Yeah, he'll be there soon," she says and then disconnects the call.

I sit down on the curb and stare at the number thirty. Thirty texts. Thirty chances to read disappointment.

My phone dings. Guess that's thirty-one now.

Regina – I'm super pissed at you

I stare at my phone for what feels like five minutes straight. Of course she's mad. I would be too.

I try taking some deep breaths, but it's hard. *Suck it up, Tori, and write the text.*

Me – I know

Regina – you shouldn't have run

I drag my fingers through my hair.

Regina – but Dani was way outta line

Regina – you crushed Nick

I rub at the ache building in my chest.

Regina – fix this

A bitter laugh escapes my lips, making me sound like the unhinged person my mom believes I am. Fix this? Has she not realized how screwed up I am? What does she expect me to do? Just thinking about going to school on Wednesday makes me want to run screaming.

Wednesday.

What kind of hell is that going to bring?

* * *

The last couple of days have consisted of watching a ridiculous amount of reality TV and dodging text messages. But I'm here at school. And you would think I slept with the whole football team and murdered the school's mascot with the looks I'm getting. Deep breaths. I can do this. I can do this.

Who am I kidding? I can't do this. This is the beginning of some sad TV show. Any minute they're all going to yell at me. Dr. West was so wrong, homeschooling sounds like an excellent idea. I turn back to the exit.

"Tori?"

So. Close.

I turn around and see Mrs. Martha poking her head out of her office door. At least she doesn't have a look of pure venom on her face. I head over to her and on my way I'm pretty sure I just see the gym teacher make a spitting noise at me from down the hall. Really?

"Come in my office before they break out the firewood," she tells me, her face completely serious.

"What?" I ask, following her inside.

She flaps her hand around in the air, totally nonchalant. "You know—for building a bonfire."

"Isn't that for witches?"

"I think it was for anyone they didn't like. Witchcraft was just an excuse."

Fantastic.

"I assume everyone knows?" I ask.

"It's a small school, and Zack was a pretty beloved guy."

I purse my lips; I figured that over the past two months. "So, why are they going to break out the firewood?"

She motions me to sit down. Of course, it's next to the creepy Gene Simmons doll. She really needs to get rid of that thing. "People are angry, confused, and sad about Zack. And because you knew and kept it secret, they're turning all those perfectly normal feelings toward *you*. It's not right. They should be wondering why his parents didn't tell them, or even how they didn't see this coming. But grief and logic don't usually coexist. You make an easy target for them to focus on right now, rather than the reality of their loss."

Well, this sucks for me. "I'm waiting for a riot to start."

"I'm going to be honest: today, and probably the rest of the week, is going to be bad."

I cock an eyebrow. Tell me something I don't know.

"But you have to suck it up," she says.

My jaw drops. She raises her hand, cutting me off. "I know it sounds harsh. A lot of people are angry, but you need to worry about yourself. You need to find a way to keep strong in your classes and walking through the halls. It'll be hard, but push through it."

I laugh. "A lot easier said than done, Mrs. Martha."

"Yup, but sometimes life sucks. Sometimes it's amazing, and sometimes it's boring. Life is never easy."

"It never is," I whisper.

I can't believe I'm being so candid with her. Must be because I'm still in shock, right?

"Are you ready to go out there?" she asks.

"No."

"The bell is about to ring and I'm not writing you a late pass. So put on your big-girl panties and get going."

I walk out of her office just when the warning bell rings. Everyone is too busy rushing down the halls to notice me. That changes as soon as I get into homeroom, though. The worst thing is the whispers. Sometimes I'd rather someone be mean right to my face. Not knowing what's being said behind those hands is so much worse.

I find my seat and slink into it, staring straight ahead at the white board. Trying to ignore everyone around me. But the whispers pick up in volume.

"I can't believe she knew and didn't tell anyone."

"Poor Nick."

"Did you know she tried to kill herself?"

The last one is too much for me.

I bolt from my seat and rush to the door.

"Victoria," Mr. Knell calls after me.

"Yeah, I'm done," I yell as I run past him. I pull out my phone and send an SOS to Dr. West. Guess I'm not making it till Monday.

29

____

"TELL ME WHAT HAPPENED AT SCHOOL," DR. WEST SAYS.

My breath stutters. After telling her about John, I had this fear lingering that it would change our meetings. I'm not ready to talk about more. I don't know if I'll ever be. And even though school was hell today, I'd still rather talk about things happening right now versus what happened last year. "I left before they broke out the pitchforks."

She tilts her head to the side and her eyebrows scrunch a bit. "Never mind, I'm not sure I want to know," she says, waving her hand in the air.

"It's better than the 'being the football team slut' analogy I came up with earlier," I mutter to myself.

A surprised bark of laughter leaves the doc. "Well, I'm glad you can find some humor in this," she says. "Even if it's a little dark."

"It's either laugh or cry. I've done enough crying."

She leans back in her chair. "Tell me about Zack wanting Nick to hand out the envelopes."

All right, guess we're diving right in. "Yeah. He said that each contained a piece of his heart for his friends."

"Has Nick asked about them?" She's totally fishing right now.

I look down at my hands. "No, I haven't talked to him since he saw the video."

"Have you tried?" Her tone is earnest, which I am so thankful for right now. I can't handle anymore judgement today.

"No," I whisper, ashamed. He texted once, but it's just been one word: *why*. But like every other text I got, I ignored it.

She sits in her chair patiently, no doubt waiting for me to explain.

"I don't know what to tell him. I don't even know if he would listen to me."

She props her chin up with her fist. "You like him, right? You're friends?"

"I think so, but it's not that easy. I'm able to relax around him, but I still have a hard time if he touches me. And with everything that's happened, I don't know where I stand with him anymore. But ultimately, it might not even matter. I feel like a lost cause. Like I'm too broken and not worth anyone's effort."

"Tori, don't you see how far you've come?"

I shake my head, not following her.

She places her hands flat on the desk and leans toward me. "You're able to be alone with Nick. You admit he puts you at ease. You've opened up to me. These are huge steps. You still have work to do, but you're headed down a very good path."

I never really thought of that.

"Tell me: do you want a relationship with a guy someday?" she asks.

Do I? Sometimes I miss things like going on dates or holding someone's hand. I miss the exciting feeling in my stomach when I like a guy and he likes me back. And at times, I've felt those things around Nick. "Yes."

"Then let's keep doing the work, so when you're ready, you can be confident in a relationship. The healthiest relationship begins as friends. And being friends with guys like Nick is a good start."

"I don't even know if we're still friends." The doubt is unmistakable in my voice.

"You need to talk to him. Not only is he hurting because he realized he lost his best friend, he also needs you to share everything with him about what you found. Is he going to be mad at you? Probably, but from what you've told me about him, he sounds like someone capable of forgiveness."

"But what do I do?" I plead.

"Call him, stop by his house, maybe take him to see Zack's special room."

I never thought I would have to share that space, but it seems fitting that Nick should see it. "Okay, I think I can do that."

"Good, now what do you want to do about Dani?"

It doesn't take me long to answer. "I don't think I can go back to being friends with her. I don't trust her, and she didn't show Nick that video out of concern. She did it out of anger and I'm pretty sure jealousy." She shouldn't be jealous. Because I'm a hot mess right now.

"Well, let's tackle one thing at a time. Dani can wait. First, talk with Nick. Do you have a class with him tomorrow?"

The thought of going back to school absolutely terrifies me. "I don't want to go back," I say in a small voice.

Dr. West purses her lips in sympathy. "I'm not going to lie. It's going to be hard. But you've learned that you can't run away anymore. You have to face your problems. You need to face your other friends too."

"Do you think they're going to blame themselves for Zack's suicide?"

"They might."

"But why?" I ask.

"It's human nature to think we could have stopped something

from happening. I'm positive your mom still feels guilt for not seeing the change in you sooner."

"It wasn't her fault," I whisper.

"No, it wasn't. But as a parent she remembers things that she saw in you that were warning signs. At the time, she might not have realized it, but looking back she does now. It's typical to feel guilt in such a situation."

That explains the compulsive hovering for the past year.

"Have you considered telling your mom about what happened with John?"

I can't stop the flinch at his name. And it makes me cringe at how weak I must seem. It's just a damn name. Four letters. Four stupid letters. And yet they make my nerves shudder and my insides heave.

"You're stronger than you know, Tori. And someday, maybe you'll feel comfortable enough to talk to your mom or Britney, or any of the others about your own suicide attempt."

I shake my head. Definitely not now, and I don't know if ever. As it is, I doubt anyone is even going to talk to me when I go to school tomorrow.

"After school tomorrow, I want you to come back and see me. I'm here for you to unload on, and I have a feeling you're going to need it," she says.

* * *

Today sucks. And not just an ordinary sucky day. It's like a pizza-was-never-created kind of sucky day. And that would be a crime of epic proportions. And it's reduced me to what I'm doing now.

The toilet next to me flushes.

Yeah, this is freaking awesome. Should have hid in the library. It would have saved my now-violated nostrils. But I couldn't take the stares and whispers anymore. Hence why I skipped homeroom.

The bell rings, but I wait. I can't do auto class today. How? How am I supposed to go in there and be partners with Nick like nothing's happened? What if Nick can't stand the sight of me—or worse, what if he doesn't look at me at all?

Unfortunately, I can't hide forever. My teachers are only going to be patient with me for so long.

I unfurl my legs and then leave the stall. I scrub my hands in the sink, part wasting time, part because hello, school bathrooms.

The late bell rings as I approach the door to auto. I stare through the little window, searching.

"He's not here." I nearly scream bloody murder at the deep voice behind me. I swing around and come face to face with Mr. Jack. He takes a step back, giving me my space.

"It's going to be bad," I say more to myself then him.

"Only if you let it."

We stand there for a moment looking through the window together. "You ready?" he asks.

"Not really."

"Sorry. Time to go, anyway." He opens the door and holds it, waiting for me to walk in first. Nothing like making a grand entrance. I make my way to my seat. It doesn't feel right that I'm sitting here and Nick isn't. He loves this class. And I can't help but feel that this is just another thing I've taken from him.

"Hey, Tori," Rossi says from behind me, and my skin crawls at the sound of his voice. "I love me some crazy chicks. I bet you're a freak in—"

"Rossi!" Mr. Jack's voice booms through the room, startling everyone to quiet.

"Get your"—he pauses and takes a body-shuddering breath—"butt up here."

Rossi slinks to the front of the room. Mr. Jack tries to whisper, but parts slip through. "...enough, if you...I'm going to...the office...fail you. You're...unacceptable, show...respect."

I feel everyone's eyes on me, making me blush. Rossi's getting chewed out because of me. *No. Rossi is getting chewed out because the guy's a dick.*

Rossi walks back to his seat, ignoring me. Thank goodness. But the atmosphere in the class has changed. No one is talking at all. I slump down in my seat and open my notebook.

Mr. Jack starts to talk about crankshafts, connecting pins, and something called a flywheel. Instead of paying attention, I cover my notebook with stars and trees. This day just needs to be over.

30

"How bad was today?" Dr. West asks as soon as I sit across from her.

"I ate lunch in a bathroom stall."

Her face shifts from professional to totally grossed out. Can't blame her. It's something I'm hoping I'll never have to do again. Best not to even think about it.

"Well, I'm proud of you for going to school today. Did you talk with any of your friends?"

I shake my head. "No. Britney hasn't been at school. Regina keeps trying to talk to me, but I'm not sure I'm ready for that conversation." Hence lunch in the bathroom and hiding in my hoodie.

"And what about Nick?"

"He wasn't there today."

Dr. West looks worried. "You need to go to him. He needs to hear from you—"

I rub at the scars on my wrists, shaking my head at her words.

"Tori." She moves around her desk and sits in the chair next to me. "He might be dealing with dark thoughts. You have some of the answers he needs. And for both of you to heal, you need to talk with him."

"But—"

"It's going to be hard. It's going to be painful. But think of all the hard things you've already done. You've lived the hardest day of your life and you're still here. This is how you start taking back your control."

"I'll try."

Dr. West looks so proud. "That's all I'll ever ask of you."

* * *

Okay, so just walk down the sidewalk, up the steps, and ring the doorbell. That's all I have to do. But why aren't my legs moving? I shift the box in my arms and look down at my feet. This box was in the attic with Nick's name on it, and it's filled with so many things and envelopes with all his friends' names on it. I have a feeling I know what's written in them, but I need to give it to Nick. Why is it so hard to move? Nothing is holding me to the cement. Deep breath. I can do this. I'm just going to the door.

I'm still standing here.

A curtain in the upstairs window shifts—I've been spotted. Can't run back home now.

I trudge to the front door and it opens before I even have the chance to ring the bell. Nick stands there, his hair a mess, and not in a just-ran-my-hands-through-it way. His eyes have lost the warmth and humor they usually have.

"I don't—" My voice cracks. "I don't have a good explanation. I'm sorry. But these are the things that Zack wanted you to have."

Nick's whole body flinches when I say his best friend's name.

"I'll answer any questions you have," I tell him in a timid voice.

His gaze finally shifts from the box to my face and his haunted expression makes me lose whatever confidence I have left. I set the box down on the step and turn to walk back down the steps. But there's one more thing I need to offer him before I can leave.

"He had a secret room up in that attic. I'm not sure if you knew about that. I want to show you it. If you want to see it, that is."

He looks at my face, and I don't understand the fleeting look that passes through his eyes. Maybe the attic was another secret Zack kept. He picks up the box and turns back into the house. He shuts the door carefully—I thought for sure he would have slammed it. The click of the lock is the saddest sound I've heard all day.

I walk away from his house, my breathing labored. My hands start to shake, and I know what's coming. Freaking panic attack. I need to breathe.

I take in a small breath as I walk toward home. It's not really working that great, because Nick's face flashes in my mind, but somehow, I get myself home.

* * *

My mom's "guest voice" floats up the stairs: overly cheerful and way too excited.

"Victoria, Nick's here to see you." The cheerfulness is suddenly forced. She knows some of what's going on from Kris. She knows Dani likes Nick and that Dani and I aren't talking right now, but I'm not sure how much more she knows.

I hesitantly walk to the top of the stairs. I didn't think I'd see him a couple hours after dropping the box off. I finally see him, and he looks haggard and lost. The box I gave him sits in his arms. His spark is still gone. And a pain fills the pit of my stomach. I had a hand in making those dead eyes.

"Why don't you come upstairs?" I ask.

My mom asks me with her eyes if I need anything, and I shake my head. Even if I did, the wringing of her hands is enough for me to just soldier on and pretend everything is okay. I turn and walk into my room. Nick stops at my door and whatever composure he had a minute ago with my mom is obliterated. And I wonder if that's what my eyes look like usually—dead and drained.

I rub at my cuffs. "Sorry, I didn't...this is the only place we can talk without my mom hovering."

His eyes scan the things in my room, probably comparing it to what it looked like when it was Zack's.

I let him have his fill. There's not much to see; I haven't been able to bring myself to decorate it.

He sets the box down on my desk, his focus trained on the broken mirror in the corner.

"Where did you find his things?" His voice is rough, like he hasn't used it in days.

I point above us. "The attic wasn't touched. I don't think his parents remembered about his space in the attic. They left everything up there."

Nick turns to the closet. "I forgot," he says, but it's like he's not talking to anyone but himself. He moves toward it, and I stand motionless in the middle of my room. Do I follow him? I don't know what to do or how to act around him.

Before he disappears into the closet, he glances back to me. "Do you mind?"

I shake my head and follow him in. If he doesn't want me to come, I'm sure he'll tell me.

We start to climb, and his voice carries reverently through the small space. "We used to play up here as kids all the time. I didn't know he still used this space."

I let him talk because I'm not sure what else to do for him. He turns the light on, and a pained gasp escapes his lips. He brings his fist to his mouth and bites it as silent tears stream down his cheeks.

The sight of those tears makes my heart falter. I never thought I'd watch another person break, but I am. And the broken shards of sorrow filling my heart are almost more than I can bear.

He crouches down, like he can't handle the weight of his emotions anymore. "Zack." That name is filled with all the anguish of a tortured heart.

He finally locks eyes with me. "Why—" His voice breaks. "Why would someone kill themself? Why did you try?"

My stomach drops. Could he have picked a more loaded question? I make my way over to the desk; I can't look at him when I tell him this. "Do you want to know why I chose to do it or what caused it?" My heart beats wildly in my chest. I wipe my nervous palms on my jeans.

"Both," he whispers.

I sit down in the lone chair and focus on the portrait on the desk. Zack's broken eyes stare back at mine. Nick's body hovers close behind mine, but I don't turn. I can't look at him during this. "His name was John; he was my boyfriend. He thought that meant he got to do whatever he wanted with my body. Whether I wanted him to or not."

My breathing picks up in speed, but I need to get this out. "After it happened, I couldn't deal. I couldn't handle how much I hated myself for not fighting more. I couldn't look at myself in the mirror. Every time I thought about that night, it made me sick. And he dumped me as well. And you would have thought that would have made me feel better, but I felt like trash. Like life was spiraling so fast, so out of control, that I just wanted it all to stop. How could I keep going when I felt like nothing? John tossed me aside like trash. I didn't want to live with the shame and guilt that smothered me. I didn't want to live anymore."

I finally work up the courage to look at him. His eyes hold mine. Anger simmers there. "And now?" he asks.

I look down at my wrists. How do I feel now? I think I know, but how do I make him understand? "Every day is different. Some days seem fine, but lately they're hard. But I don't know if I could do that to my mom and dad again. That's the thing about suicide; in that moment you're not really thinking about the ones you're leaving behind."

"I'm so mad at him."

"Zack?" I ask.

He slashes a hand through the air. "Yeah. Why didn't he come to me? Why didn't he tell someone? I knew he was having a hard time after Britney, but this? How could he just leave me? What about the rest of us that are still here?"

I take a deep breath. "I'm not him, but I know he wasn't thinking straight. In that moment, everything gets clouded. You're not thinking of tomorrow, you're thinking of ending the pain right then and there. You know, my dad said he felt something was wrong with me, but he thought it would pass. He always tells me that he wishes he had spoken up or pushed the issue.

"Depression is so hard to explain. It's not just sadness. It's not just crying. It's this feeling of helplessness. Of being utterly alone. Of wanting something that's always just out of reach. It's feeling worthless and ridiculous all at the same time. And it's not constant. It's not every day. But sometimes it sneaks up on you and you're leveled."

I rake my fingers through my hair.

"You *know* the thoughts that swarm your mind are wrong and misplaced, but they keep coming until you can't take it anymore, so you isolate yourself, either physically or emotionally. Until the weight of those thoughts crushes whatever spirit you have left."

The honesty of my words hangs in the room, echoing around all the dark, dusty corners. It's easier to tell him what depression isn't versus what it is.

"I just wish..." he begins, and then his sad eyes turn back to me. "Why didn't you tell me sooner? About Zack?"

I swallow the large ball of guilt blocking my throat. He deserves all my honesty. "At times I feared it would change you. I didn't want to see the life die in your eyes. I didn't want to see your eyes turn into mine."

He runs his hands roughly through his hair, gripping the ends. "I needed to know."

"I know that now. I wanted to tell you. But as we got to know each other better, it got harder to figure out how to tell you. The longer I waited, the worse it got. I'm sorry about how you found out. I'd give anything to change that. No one should learn such devastating news in such a heartless way."

He looks back toward the ladder. "I haven't touched the box. I haven't been able to face it."

"Do you want to now?"

His body deflates. "Not really. But I know I need to, and I don't want to do it alone."

I get that. He walks back to the ladder, and I follow him down the rungs and back into my bedroom.

With determined strides he moves for the box on my bed. He sits down next to it and I take a seat in my desk chair and roll it next to the bed.

He swallows a couple times. "Can you play the video again for me?"

I lightly touch the top of my laptop. Without the paper I can't find it anymore. I deleted everything from my internet history. "I don't have access to it."

He pulls the small slip of paper out of his pocket and holds it out to me. Dani must have given it to him. She probably thought she was helping. I'm still so angry with her. I push that aside. I need to focus on Nick. I open the computer and type in the address. Zack's face, the one I've come to know, fills the screen. Nick's face crumbles as he listens to his best friend. I reach out and grab his hand. And I hold it tight as he falls apart watching his friend's goodbye.

The video stops. A heavy silence fills my room. It's broken from the sobbing on the other side of the door.

Mom.

31

"You better go out there," Nick says, eyeing my bedroom door.

Without thinking, I hand the computer to Nick and open my door. She's sitting on the hallway floor across from my room. I kneel in front of her.

"Was that the boy who used to live here?" she asks through heaving breaths.

"Yes," I tell her.

Her bottom lip trembles. "It sounded so much like your letter." Her voice sounds lost like a child's.

"I read that letter over and over when you were in the hospital. Wishing you would survive, wanting to shake you, wanting to never let you go. I wanted to tell you that life is never easy or fair, but just to make the best out of what you're given. That your family loves you no matter what. And then I wanted to pretend nothing bad ever happened. I wanted to forget."

My heart stalls at the honesty in her words. We haven't talked this openly since months before I tried committing suicide.

She finally looks me in the eye. "I think it's time we work on being a family again and get back to really talking."

I try to smile. "Okay, Mom." The guilt floods me like a tidal wave washing out my emotions. How does one work on being a family again? Every time I think we're getting there, something throws us off. I thought we were getting back to normalcy the morning we had French toast. But that feels like months ago, even though it wasn't.

She wipes the tears from her face and looks toward the room. "You have an insight he needs. I'm glad you're helping him." With that, she stands and heads back down the stairs.

I walk back to Nick, and he's staring at Zack's face on my computer screen. "Everything your mom said is true."

I sink onto the bed beside him. "Since it happened, my mom either pretends nothing ever happened or is magically fine, or she's hovered like I might try it again at any minute. That's the first real conversation we've had in over a year."

He looks at me with those dead eyes. "You weren't the only one that got hurt."

"I know that now," I say. I know that more than he'll ever know.

He turns back to the screen and shakes his head. "I don't know what to do now."

I hate how lost he is because I know how it feels. Then a crazy —and I mean super crazy—idea pops into my head. There's only been one person who's been able to really help me. "Well, if you want, you can come talk to my"—I struggle to get the next word out—"therapist."

"You see one here, in Saybrooke?"

I look away. "Yes."

He tugs my sleeve and I flinch a little, but he ignores it. Instead, he says, "Hey, that's a good thing. Maybe if Zack saw someone, he'd still be here."

"If you want, you can come with me sometime and talk to her."

A sad smile tugs at his lips. "Maybe."

I blow out a huge breath. "Okay." I point at the box. "Are you going to hand those out like he asked?"

His shoulders slump. "It's what he wanted. And he asked me; I can't say no."

"I could help you." His eyes jerk to mine—wait! What is wrong with me? Did I just offer that? Everyone at the school hates me right now. "On second thought—"

"I'd like that," he tells me, his face softer now.

"I'm not really everyone's favorite person right now."

He shrugs like it isn't a big deal. "Maybe not, but I'd like your help."

"I'm sure Dani would help." Wow, that came out a lot snarkier than I meant it to.

"I haven't talked to Dani since she showed this to me," he says, gesturing toward the computer.

"Really?"

"I was so mad at you at first...still am, a bit. For not telling me yourself." His words sting, but I don't blame him for his anger. "But Dani should have told me a different way. At least in private. She did that to be hurtful toward you and it wasn't right."

"I should have told you sooner," I say. "I hope you'll forgive me someday." Maybe having him come sometime with me to Dr. West will help fix my mistake.

And maybe talking with her can relieve some of the guilt currently drowning me.

"Come with me Friday to hand these out?" he asks, looking so unlike the confident guy I've come to know.

"I'll be there."

* * *

"He came to my house." I don't even bother with a hello to Dr.

West. My nerves are shot, my mind feels like it's on a constant loop, and I want to throw up.

"Nick?"

"Yeah." I try controlling my knee, but it has a mind of its own, and it wants to rattle the whole desk. But Dr. West is a pro and ignores it.

"I'm proud of you for reaching out to him—"

"My mom overheard us talking," I interrupt. I don't want her pride. I don't deserve her accolades. I get up from the chair and start pacing back and forth. All these things are rising up in me. I thought I had a better handle on it.

"What did she—"

"When will this"—I jab at the hollowed-out spot in my chest—"not feel so empty? And when will my mind stop working against me and start working *with* me? When will I not be so broken?"

I hate the desperation falling from my lips. I hate the feeling of not being in control. Haven't I been working on this emptiness within me? Why am I not better?

"You have to fight to fill your heart and your mind with truth and love. Piece by piece. You must accept that it's okay when your brain chemistry is thrown off and your body needs help to correct it. You aren't alone to do that. We'll keep working together in here. But you aren't alone outside of this office, either. Your parents love you and want to help; you have friends that are still sticking by you in what you thought would sever the friendships you've made. You're not that broken girl anymore, Tori."

My fists pound on her desk. "But I am!"

"Enough."

One word said so calmly, but it's a command. And I throw myself back into the chair, obeying.

Dr. West stares at me, perplexed. "Where is this really coming from? What are you thinking about right now?"

"Every time I feel like maybe I'm...better? I don't know. More in control? Every time I get to that point, something comes and knocks me back down. I told Nick. I *told* him. He wanted to know why I did what I did, so I told him. But his eyes. The light is gone. And then my mom..."

"Tell her."

"I can't." My voice is so small. My mom already struggles with how she acts around me. If I tell her this. If I tell her I was...raped —I can hardly think the word—it'll break her more.

"You *are not* that broken girl. He will not hurt you again."

"But why do I feel like I could have stopped him?"

"Never take the blame for this. He and he alone chose not to listen when you said stop. He took what you weren't willing to give, without your consent. This will never be your fault. And like I keep telling you, one day, even if you don't believe it now, you'll see that."

A weary sigh leaves my lips. "How do I tell my mom?" I ask.

"You could bring her here or take her somewhere you feel comfortable. And remember, your mom is a strong woman. Don't try and shield her from a world she might already know about. But trust me. It might change things between you more than you know."

"I'll think about it."

But first, I promised Nick I would help him hand out Zack's letters at the school.

32

"FREAKING LIFETIME MOVIE," I SAY AS WE GET OUT OF HIS CAR IN the school's parking lot. It's too early on a Friday morning for the amount of drama headed our way.

"Lifetime?" Nick asks.

"You know, those overly dramatic movies made for TV. I feel like any minute a soul-crushing song is going to start playing, everything will slow down, and everyone in school will turn and stare at us."

He looks toward the school. "Well, everyone *is* staring at us."

Perfect.

"I could play some music on my phone if you want. Maybe some Novo Amor?" he asks, completely serious.

A surprise laugh escapes me.

Nick's lips lift in a quasi-smile, but it's fleeting. "I wouldn't do that again. Everyone really is looking now."

I glance around; he's right. A part of me wants to grab his hand, but a bigger part is mortified by the idea. Not to mention he's trying to cheer me up when really it should be the other way around.

Just need to breathe and regroup. "So, you sent the text?" I ask after taking a couple deep breaths. It's been hit or miss on who's been at school.

"Yup. They're meeting us on the steps."

"Good, nice and public. Wide open. No pig's blood."

"Pig's blood?" He sounds completely confused. Kind of have that effect on people I suppose.

"You know, *Carrie*? Prom? Doused in pig's blood?"

He rolls his eyes. "No more intense movies for you. How about you stick with Disney for a while."

"Really? Disney? Those things are full of drama. Someone's parent dies or is already dead in most of them. Don't even get me started on the heartbreak of *The Lion King*."

His rich laughter fills the air around us, and I feel some pride knowing I brightened his eyes, even if only for a minute. "Didn't know you were a closet Disney fanatic, Tori."

I lift my shoulders. "Isn't that a given growing up in America?"

Any response he might give is sucked back with a breath as we get closer to the school's steps. Guess our time has come.

"What are you doing with *her*?" Dani asks. Her arms are crossed over her chest and her usually pretty face is twisted into a sneer.

Nick grabs my hand. I stiffen and have to work very hard not to snatch it back. He needs this right now. Dani's eyes hone in on our hands. Her hands drop to her sides and clench into tight fists.

"Enough, Dani," Nick says, sounding so tired with her.

"You asked us here. What's the deal?" Doug asks Nick, not really looking at me.

Nick's grip on my hand tightens. "It's about Zack," he says.

No one says anything for a moment, but all their faces shut down.

"He wanted"—I clear my suddenly dry throat—"he wanted you guys to have something."

"Don't you dare talk about him like you know him," Dani shouts at me.

"What did he leave?" Britney asks in a quiet voice, completely ignoring Dani.

"Really, Britney?" Dani whines. "How do you know she's not lying? She didn't tell us about him in the first place. Maybe she's making this up now. We can't trust a word she says."

Regina steps away from Dani and throws her arm around Britney. "Drop it, Dani. Nick wouldn't be here with her if it wasn't the truth," she says.

"I can't believe you guys," Dani says. And I'm assuming she hasn't stormed off yet because she wants to see what we have.

"So, what is it?" Britney asks again. She hasn't taken her eyes off of Nick.

Nick looks at me. I really wish he would take over now. But I'm the one who found everything. I waited and didn't tell anyone. I can hear Dr. West right now congratulating me for owning up to my actions.

"Zack had a secret space in the attic. I found the entrance one day in the back of my closet. It's filled with all his art and pictures. That's where I found the slip of paper with the link to his message. And that's where he left letters for all of you." I motion to Nick's backpack.

Nick releases my hand and reaches for his bag. He pulls out the envelopes and passes them out. Britney takes hers and runs her fingertips over her name. Her shoulders start to shake. Maybe we shouldn't have done this at school. Tears stream down her cheeks now. Yeah, definitely should have found somewhere else to do this.

"We haven't read any, so I have no clue what's inside," Nick tells them.

He stretches his hand out to Dani and she rips the envelope

out of his hand. She pierces me with a venomous glare and then turns and stomps away.

"Don't worry about her," Regina says to Nick. "She's madder about you and Tori than anything else."

I sigh; this is way past ridiculous now. "Have you talked with her?" I ask Nick.

"No," he says.

"Maybe you should," I add.

He looks in the direction of where she stormed off to, but he doesn't move.

"Don't worry about me," I say. "No buckets of pig's blood in sight."

"Pig's blood?" Regina asks, horrified.

Both Nick and I ignore her. "I'm not ready to talk to her yet," Nick says. "I don't even think she knows what she did was wrong."

The sound of sniffles stops our conversation. Britney hugs her envelope to her chest. And I feel like such a jerk that I was joking about pig's blood instead of paying attention to her. I don't know what it's like to learn the boy you've loved is gone from this earth. I walk over to her and wrap my arms around her. She crushes the envelope between us.

"Why?" she sobs into my shoulder. "Please, you need to tell me why. You know. You *know*."

Maybe it's time I tell more people parts of my story. Even though Zack and I aren't the same, maybe my thoughts will help them. It won't bring him back. It won't change the fact that there will never be another Zack in this world, but maybe it can help them heal.

I hold her, letting her tears soak my shirt. I watch Regina crumple into Doug's arms, and Nick looks off into the distance. What a mess this is. Every one of them needs to go see Dr. West, but I doubt she'd let us all pile into her office.

"Tori?" I turn at the sound of Mrs. Martha's voice as she walks out the front door. "Is everything all right?"

I lift my head, but Britney still clutches me tightly to her. "I think some of us really need to talk with you right now," I tell her, and I shift my eyes to Britney.

She walks closer to Britney, placing a hand on her shoulder. "Would you like to come to my office? You can sit and relax; talk or not talk. Regina, Gretchen, you can come too."

Britney steps backs and nods at Mrs. Martha. Both she and Regina follow Mrs. Martha into the school. Doug rocks back on his heels as he watches them go. He blows out a breath and finally looks back at us. "I can't do school today. I'm going to take off."

"You want us to go with you?" Nick asks.

"No. I need to be alone when I read this," he says, holding up the envelope.

Nick walks over and they do a quick embrace. "All right, man, text me later. We're all going to need each other."

Doug gives him a tight smile and heads for the parking lot. I watch him go, noting that he never looked at me the entire time I've been standing here. But I can't dwell on that. That's an issue I just don't have the mental space for right now.

Nick and I stand there for a moment, still frozen. "That's not how I thought this would go down." His eyes stay trained on where the girls walked into the school.

"I don't know if we could ever predict how they would react to this news. And I don't think this would ever be easy."

His weary eyes finally meet mine. "Let's get you home."

* * *

A hesitant knock on my bedroom door has me rolling over. The door slowly creaks open, and it isn't my mom on the other side. I rub at my eyes because there's no way *she* would show up here

188

after how she acted a couple of hours ago in the school parking lot.

"Dani?" I bolt up in my bed.

"I'm sorry," Dani says, her eyes filling with unshed tears. She hovers in the doorway like she's afraid to come any closer.

I want to scream at her for bringing unnecessary pain to our friends. Spew all the anger within me at her for breaking a trust we've had since we were babies. But it isn't all her fault. I kept secrets—life-altering ones.

But some things I can't forget, and I'm having a hard time forgiving.

"You just accused me of lying about all of Zack's letters. You screamed, in front of the whole school, that I tried to kill myself," I say to her, barely controlling the urge to shake her.

My eyes snag on her throat as she swallows, but I keep going.

"You told everyone something that wasn't your place to tell," I say, letting the pain bleed into my voice.

Her head falls toward her chest.

"And I know I kept secrets I shouldn't have," I admit, "but once you found out you should have come to me first. Instead of finding a way to ease the agony this brought, you shattered people. You broke and destroyed everyone because you were jealous."

Her shoulders start to shake, and the sobs she's trying to hide slip out.

"And I'm a part of this too," I say, taking a deep breath trying to calm my out-of-control heart. "We need to fix this."

"How?" she asks as she wipes her face.

"You heard that Nick wants to do a tribute to Zack at prom, right?"

She nods.

"For starters, you should help Nick with that. But mainly, you need to talk with Nick."

She shakes her head vehemently. "He won't talk to me."

"Try," I urge her.

Her desolate, broken eyes finally meet mine. "And us?" she asks.

I look away; the anger hasn't left me yet and I'm not sure when it will. "I don't know."

An excruciating silence fills the room. And it's like I can feel the door in my mind closing our friendship. One day, I might not feel this rage toward her, but we'll never go back to what we were.

"Okay," she says, almost sounding worse than when she first got here. She turns to leave but pauses to ask, "See you at school tomorrow?"

"Yeah. I'll be there."

She nods once and leaves my room. I wonder what was in Zack's letter to make her come here so soon. But whatever words he threw on that page, I'm grateful for them, because it struck a chord in her.

33

______

I WAS SO CLOSE TO STAYING HOME FROM SCHOOL TODAY. IT'S BEEN three days since Nick and I handed the letters out and Dani showed up at my bedroom door. And even though I've texted back and forth with Nick and Regina, I'm still unsettled. I don't know what faces me when I walk into school. There are moments when I feel like I can handle it, but walking down those halls with everyone knowing I tried committing suicide... Dr. West keeps telling me I'm not broken, but I feel like I only have a little of myself glued back together and one well-placed blow is going to shatter all the work I've done.

"You ready for school, Sweets?" Dad calls from the bottom of the stairs.

I shake out my hands, suck in a deep breath, and sling my bag over my shoulder.

He's waiting for me at the bottom, keys already in hand, and I have a sudden urge to throw my arms around him. There's no way I could handle twenty questions from Mom this morning. My brain is already in fifty million places.

I grab my sweatshirt and call a goodbye to my mom as we head out the door. Her faint response is cut off with the closing of the door.

"I'm okay with you missing another day," Dad says as we slide into the car.

My seatbelt clicks into place. "Today, tomorrow, or next week... it's not going to make much difference. Might as well get it over with."

His hand hovers near the ignition button. "I don't know whether to say 'that's the spirit' or give you a hug."

I chuckle. "Me neither, Dad."

"How 'bout both?" He leans over to give me an awkward car hug. "That's the spirit, kid. Knock 'em dead today."

"Uh oh, you went off script."

He gives a cocky shrug. "Sometimes you've got to live dangerously."

A little crack in my heart melds together; it's been a while since I've seen his corny side. But I'm glad it's back.

* * *

I walk into homeroom, slightly terrified I'll run right out. Regina and Nick sit in their usual seats, their heads close together in conversation. As I walk past the threshold, the sudden silence is suffocating. It sucks. I make my way to my seat, focusing on Regina and Nick.

"How's it going?" I ask as I sit down.

"Horrible," Nick says in a muted voice.

"Sounds about right."

"Well, I'm pissed," Regina throws in. "I read his letter, but I'm still so freaking angry at him."

Nick runs a hand over his face. "We all are."

We fall silent as Mr. Knell walks into the room. He steps in front of the class, hands deep in his pockets. He rocks back on his heels. "I know it's been a tough week. I just want you all to know that our counselors are here if you need to talk. I am, too."

Every class I walk into, every teacher says the same thing. And if it weren't for how sad they all look, I would think it was just being pushed by the admin. Everyone at Saybrooke really loved Zack.

At lunch, I walk into the cafeteria, not really knowing how this is going to go. I've seen Dani in passing, but we haven't talked. Britney isn't here, but I can't blame her. Regina, Nick, Doug, Gretchen, and Dani sit at our usual table.

It's the most heartrending sight I've ever seen. I don't know how to help any of them. And I don't know if I can. But maybe there's one person who will.

I slide in the spot next to Nick and lean close. "I'm going to see Dr. West after school. Do you want to come?"

His head lifts. "Yeah," he says without hesitation. "I think I do."

* * *

"Are we supposed to lie on the couch or something?" Nick leans over and whispers to me.

See, I'm not the only one who thought that. "No. That's the first thing I asked when I came here too."

"Why does she have it, then?"

"Some people feel more comfortable lying down," Dr. West says from behind us.

Nick jumps at the sound of her voice.

"Would *you* like to lie down?" she asks.

I smile, remembering when she asked me the same thing.

"No, I'm good with the chair," he says.

"Then let's have a seat," says Dr. West.

We move over to the chairs, and I plop into my normal seat, but Nick slowly lowers himself down into his. Dr. West does her silent staring bit and I watch Nick squirm in his seat. It's so nice to have someone else on the end of that stare for a change.

"I usually don't have more than one person in a session, but Tori thought it'd be good for you to come with her. To talk about your friend Zack."

"Yeah." He shifts in his chair, his eyes sliding to mine. I have a sudden urge to give him a hug.

"I'm assuming the news of his death came as a shock?" she asks gently.

"Yeah." His throat works like he's swallowing a large ball of guilt. "I should have known something wasn't right. And then when his parents just up and moved. It was weird that he wouldn't at least get to say goodbye."

What is it about Dr. West that gets people to spill their guts in record time? She nods. "I can't speak for his parents, of course, but people cope in different ways when a child takes their own life."

Images of my mom flash before me.

Putting up those ridiculous sayings.

Watching me constantly.

Forced smiles.

Never-ending questions.

"I've known him my whole life, though. They've known me since I was a baby. How could they not tell me? His best friend?" Nick's voice rises in anger with each question.

"Who are you really mad at?" Dr. West asks.

Nick grips the arms of his chair. I watch as his knuckles whiten and the veins become more pronounced. "What are you talking about?" he asks. But it sounds more like an accusation than a genuine question.

"It's okay to be mad at Zack."

He jerks back like she slapped him.

"Is it?" he asks. He doesn't believe her.

"Of course it is. It doesn't change how you feel about him. It doesn't change the memories you cherish. Your feelings matter, too—whether he's still here to hear them or not."

Air rushes past his lips in a loud huff. "He left. He killed himself and left me to pick up the pieces. He left without even thinking about me or Britney or any of our friends. He told me I'd be fine. But I'm not fine. How could I be fine with the fact that my best friend killed himself? How could he be so selfish?"

Each word he says is a slash at my heart. Each word could be meant for me.

My eyes, now wet, drift toward Dr. West. "This is what you wanted me to hear, isn't it? Why you agreed to have Nick come?" I ask, my voice sounding so sad even to my own ears.

I can feel Nick's eyes on me even though I don't stop looking at Dr. West. "This is a unique situation that presented itself. This is how things would have been if your mom hadn't found you in time," she tells me gently.

"But my mom has never shown anger toward me. She's never shouted. She walks around like I'm going to break any minute."

"Like I said before: everyone deals with grief in different ways and stages. She may never rant and rave at you, but that doesn't mean she hasn't felt anger. But the feelings Nick has, they are normal."

Her gaze swings back to Nick, but I can't look at him right now. "It's good to have these feelings—even healthy. A grief like this won't heal in one day, though. It might help for you to talk with your parents about coming to see me again sometime or seeing another therapist. I can give you names."

"Yeah, that'd be nice."

"Good. Do you mind stepping out and giving Tori and me a minute?"

"Sure," he says, and shoots me a tiny smile.

As soon as the door closes, Dr. West focuses on me. "I know it wasn't easy hearing all of that, but I'm proud of you for listening. Now, have you had a chance to talk with your mom?"

"No," I confess, averting my eyes.

"I really want you to consider it."

"I'll take it under advisement, Doc."

"That's all I ask."

34

———

I NEVER TOLD MY MOM ABOUT WHAT HAPPENED WITH JOHN. THE whole time we were dating she probably only met him twice. But after... Sometimes I hope that maybe if I forget about it, it'll be like it didn't happen. But I never forget it. It haunts me. It's this presence that's sucking the life out of me. I'm exhausted. And maybe it's dumb, but I don't know why I think my mom would be disappointed in me if she knows what really happened. Sometimes I feel like I should have been stronger. Dr. West's words keep swirling around in my mind, but they haven't stuck yet.

I watch my mom now, typing away on her computer at the kitchen table.

"Mom?"

"Yeah, baby," she says without looking up from whatever she's typing.

I hesitate in the doorway. There's still time to leave. But the words *I don't want to live like this anymore* shoot through my mind like a missile.

"Uh..." How do I even do this? How do I explain to her the darkness that lingers within?

She closes her computer and gives me her full attention. Her face morphs into forced cheer, but her eyes are wary.

"Dr. West said..."

My wrists start burning, and I can't stop rubbing at my cuff. It's like my body is fighting against me. I can't do it.

I don't even realize she crossed the room until her warm hand covers mine. "Do you want to tell me what led to that night?" Her voice is laced with anguish.

I clear my throat a few times and nod. "A few weeks—" My voice struggles, so thick with fear and nerves. I clear my throat and continue. "A few weeks before I tried..." *This is so hard.*

She squeezes my hand. "Whatever it is, it won't change how much I love you."

"Mom, I was raped." The words go off like a gunshot.

Her grip becomes almost painful, but in a way, it anchors me. She pulls until I fall into her arms. She wraps me in a hug and strokes my hair like I'm little again. "I'm so sorry, baby. I don't even have the words to tell you how sorry I am."

"I should have—"

"No," Mom cuts my off. "There are no 'should haves' or 'if onlys.' There will never be a way that it was your fault."

The tears finally burst through their dam, and I crumple into a puddle at my mom's feet. She follows me down, never letting go. And it's here on the floor that I pour out the story to her. The pain. The shame. The dark corners of my soul that I've been trying so hard to hide.

"You're so strong," she whispers to me repeatedly.

I shake my head, but she keeps repeating that I am.

She grabs my face, and it forces me to look at her. "You are seventeen and have experienced something no woman should ever have to. And I know you wanted to give up. I held you in my arms that night. And I felt you fading. But I want you to stay. There is no one in this world like you, Tori, and there never will be again. Stay. Become all that you are meant to be."

Her tears run freely, and she doesn't bother to wipe them away.

"Some days it's unbearable to be around people who are so happy and so put together, and I can't be that. I can't feel that."

Her hand gently brushes my cheek. "Baby. Everyone has their own hell they're going through. Some are just better at getting through it or hiding it. The key is to tell yourself to try again. That's all we can ask of ourselves. Try again."

I lay my head against her chest and there on the kitchen floor she rocks me, just like when I was a little girl. Maybe I'll never be a hundred percent whole. I'll never be the girl I once was. But from all of this, I know I can try again.

* * *

"I told her yesterday."

Dr. West leans back in her chair. "That was very brave of you. Every time you talk about what happened to you, you gain back a part that was taken. I'm pleased that you're owning your past, even if it's messy and uncomfortable. We're still going to work together. But I am so damn proud of the steps you're taking."

She lets us sit in a comfortable silence for the first time.

"Have you ever asked yourself what you want out of life?"

"I used to know. Then, for a while, my only goal was to make it through each breath. Until it moved to each minute, hour, day. Now...I want to find who I am. Who is *this* Tori? And when will I give her the love that she deserves?"

"We can find out together."

"Yeah. I guess we can."

* * *

Nick: Come somewhere with me?
    Me: Where?
    Nick: The lifeguard chair?
    Me: Yeah. I'll come with you.

* * *

The cool breeze wraps around us, but thankfully the harsh cold of winter has slowly loosened its grip on spring.

"Are you really not going to go to our Junior prom?" Nick asks out of nowhere.

My head jerks back. "Prom?"

He looks away from the rolling waves and settles on me, sitting next to him on the lifeguard chair. "Yeah, prom. What?"

I kick my feet back and forth over the edge of the lifeguard chair. "I just didn't see that coming."

"I was just thinking about how it's coming up in a little over a month."

"And..."

"And I want to know if you'll go to prom with me."

"Just prom?" I ask. I'm not really buying it.

"For now. I'd like to take you out on dates too, but let's start with prom."

This boy. He's been creeping into my heart little by little, but that terrifies me more than anything.

"Why? You deserve so much more; so much better. I don't know if I'll ever be what you want. I don't know if I'll ever be able to give you what you want."

He reaches over and gently takes my hand, interlocking his fingers with mine. His touch is tender. Soft. "I want you. Your snarky attitude. The smiles you reserve for me. I want your battered—not broken—heart. I want you; whole, damaged, on the mend, wherever you feel you are that day. I see you."

Tears splash on our joined hands.

"I don't see you as the girl who tried to kill herself. I see the girl who lived. I see the girl who held on and came back."

Against my will, the what-ifs swarm my mind. What if I never stop flinching when he touches me? What if I can't kiss him? What if I spiral down into another bad depression?

What if you don't? Dr. West's voice whispers in my mind.

"We've both changed, Tori. We'll never be what we once were. But I'm okay with that. I like who you are *now*. You, who had the strength to seek help, to tell me your secrets, and to face down the school."

What do you want, Tori? I hear Dr. West's voice again.

"I'd like to go to prom with you," I manage to choke out through sobs.

I take a deep, shaky breath and lightly put my arms around him, letting someone, other than family, physically comfort me for the first time in a year.

35

I STUDY THE CUFFS THAT HAVE BEEN MY NEAR-CONSTANT COMPANION for the past year. My finger glides across the leather that's hidden what I've long considered my greatest failure. The buttons unsnap easily, and I place the cuffs on my nightstand. My scars are a bit pink, the skin still noticeably puckered. But they no longer shout my greatest failure; instead, they show that I survived. And he can never take that from me.

I leave my room feeling excited and scared, and a little like I might throw up. But I don't stop; I take the first step down the stairs and then the next.

My mom gasps, pulling my attention away from the steps, and I nearly topple down the stairs in these heels. "What's wrong?" I ask and lift my hands to pat my hair. I curled it in long, soft waves —another thing I haven't done in over a year. Maybe I'm so out of practice it looks horrible.

My mom lifts her hands to her mouth and her eyes glisten. "Nothing's wrong! You look so beautiful."

My hands skate down the black lace fabric of my dress. When I told my mom that I was going to the prom, I thought she was going to pass out. She stopped breathing for a second and I had to yell her name to get her to snap out of it. The next words out her mouth were that we were going shopping, and I couldn't tell her no even though I was terrified by the idea. Now that it's here, I'm thankful we went.

What sold me on this dress was the long sleeves. The black lace hugs my body all the way to the floor, but not so tight that I can't move. I pick up the hem and walk the rest of the way down the stairs.

My mom waits for me at the bottom, taking pictures on her phone. "Mom. Enough."

"Shush and let me have this," she says. "Now lift the dress so we can see the shoes."

My dad rolls his eyes from behind her, but I still lift the dress up for her. Forest green satin heels with rhinestones adorning the toe peek out from the black satin. "Oh, these are fabulous," my mom breathes.

"All right, can I finish coming down the stairs now?" I ask after what's probably the twentieth photo. "Nick's probably going to be here soon."

Like his ears were burning, there's a knock at the front door. I try to quickly make my way down the stairs without tripping, so I can stop my dad from whatever stern lecture he wants to impart on Nick.

"Now you make sure you treat her right and—" my dad starts in, but I put a hand on his shoulder, cutting him off.

"It's okay, Dad. He's the perfect gentleman." My dad eyes Nick one more time, and then steps to the side, giving my hand a squeeze as he moves toward Mom. Nick comes into view. His eyes lock with mine and a huge smile spreads across his face.

My cheeks feel hot, but I give him a small smile back. "You look amazing," he tells me.

I fight the urge to cross my arms over my chest and hide

myself; instead, I take a deep breath and keep them at my sides. This is Nick. And he's never given me any reason to fear him.

"Thanks." I look over his crisp black tux. "You're looking pretty good yourself."

He adjusts the cuffs of his jacket and shoots me a cocky grin. "I know, right?"

My small smile spreads and a laugh bursts free.

"That's the best sound," my mom says softly.

I look over my shoulder, and she's got her body tucked into my dad's side. They look happier than I've seen them in a long time. "Have fun tonight," she says, and her eyes shift to Nick. "And good luck. It'll be hard, but I think the school needs it." He gives her a tight-lipped smile and nods once.

We pose for a few pictures before heading out to his car.

"You ready for tonight?" I ask him once we're both inside.

His knuckles turn white as he grips the steering wheel and heads toward the yacht club. "No...but we're going to do it anyway. Zack might not have asked me to do this, but it's more than just his close friends that miss him."

After the shock wore off, so many people have been in tears or have been in the counselors' office. Nick got the idea to pay tribute to his best friend at prom. Texts went out around the school, asking for anything they had about Zack. Everyone jumped on board, sending pictures, memories, videos, so many things. I was amazed at the outpour. But more than anything, I watched so many people fall apart. It was an eerie experience to see what could have been.

"I didn't know Zack, but I can see that he loved you. I think he'll be happy with whatever you do."

He reaches over and grabs my hand, giving it a firm squeeze. "I hope you're right," he says, and we keep driving to our junior prom.

36
____

NICK RUBS HIS THUMB OVER MY KNUCKLES BEFORE DROPPING IT AND walking to the mic set up onstage. He shoves his hands into his pockets and rocks back on his heels. His eyes find mine and he takes a deep breath before stepping closer to the mic.

"Less than a year ago, I thought my best friend left for military school. A week before he died, we talked about the road trip we were going to take after senior year. We even Googled where we wanted to stop in Nashville that night. I don't think either of us knew it wasn't going to happen. I mean, everyone knew about it; we'd been talking about it since the eighth grade."

He pauses and stares at the picture of Zack on the screen next to him. "Sometimes I feel like I didn't really know him. And then I think: maybe he didn't even know himself. I wish"—his voice cracks—"I wish he would have trusted me with his secrets. His pain. I wish I could have sensed how serious his cry for help was. I knew something was upsetting him. But I didn't push." He turns and his eyes touch on almost two hundred people in the room.

"I'm here tonight to tell you this: Push. Don't let what happened to Zack happen to anyone else. Don't let those signs—

205

that gut feeling that's something's wrong—just linger. Tell some-one. And if you're thinking about suicide: Stop. The world will be so much less without you. Don't leave us. Choose to stay. Don't put that grief on those who love you. My best friend is gone, and it hurts. Man does it hurt every day. I'll never get over it. I wish he was here with us being his stupid self on the dance floor like usual."

A few chuckles break out in the otherwise silent room. Nick shakes his head, a sad smile on his face. "But since he's not, we've hung his artwork around the room. Some of them he probably would never want anyone to see but...but I've been learning that depression wears a lot of different faces. Look at what he was trying to show in them, and maybe it'll touch something inside of you. I hope that if you need help or know someone that does, you'll be inspired to reach out."

He stares at the picture of Zack one more time before he leaves the mic and heads for our table.

My eyes, like everyone else's in this room, follow his slow return as the opening guitar chords of *We Don't Know* by the Strumbellas breaks the silence. On cue, a slideshow begins of all the memories that people shared with Nick over the past month.

"He'd probably hate this," Doug says.

"Yeah, well, he's not here," Nick says from beside me, anger still slowly simmering.

I place a gentle hand on his arm, and he takes a deep breath. He leans into me. "I'm going to step outside for a bit," he says into my ear.

"K. I'll be here."

He slaps Doug on the shoulder and heads for the door.

* * *

"Has she talked to you?" Regina asks.

I look across the dance floor and watch Dani dance with Doug. "Yeah. She came by my house the other day," I tell her, my eyes still following them.

"And?" Regina asks.

"And nothing. I don't know," I tell Regina. I'm not ready to make any statements. I'm not ready for thoughts to leave my mind and land on my lips. I've learned with some words, there are no take-backs.

I'm not sure what Regina sees in my face, but she nods her head. A little bit more weight shifts off my shoulders. Who knew that all I needed was a simple head nod to make that happen?

"Hey you," Nick says, his voice a little breathless. He collapses in the chair next to me.

"Hi," I say.

Britney plops down next to Regina with the first real smile I've seen in a few weeks on her face. Nick drapes his arm around the back of my chair. His thumb brushes my upper arm. My body tenses and I take a few deep breaths. I know he feels the change in my energy by the sudden increase of pressure from his thumb; but then he keeps moving it and talking with Regina. I get my body to relax in record time. I like his touch; I'm still just trying to get my body and mind in sync.

He leans over, his face close to mine. "What's it going to take for you to dance with me?" he asks.

I tap my finger against my lips. His face transforms with his beautiful smile. "Are you thinking bribery, threats, begging on my knees?" he asks.

"Oooh, I vote for begging on the knees," Regina chimes in.

"Don't." We all turn at Britney's quietly uttered word. "Don't wait. Don't play games. You don't know what tomorrow will bring. Don't live with any more regrets."

Everyone at the table goes quiet. I look down at the scars my wrists. Dr. West told me that I need to take chances on good people. And Britney's right. I am so finished with regrets. I push back my chair and stand, but Nick's already there, holding out his hand. I place mine in his and we walk out on the dance floor.

He takes both my hands and places them on his shoulders, the whole time his eyes staying locked with mine. We move to the beautiful voice of John Legend.

Nick starts to sing, but I quickly cover his mouth with my hand. "Don't ruin the moment," I tell him.

"I'm not that bad," he says, his voice muffled underneath my hand.

"Uh huh..."

"She's such an attention whore," I hear Rossi's grating voice say from close by.

"What?" Rossi's date asks.

"Tori. I bet she tried killing herself for attention."

Nick's body goes rigid.

Nope. I'm done with that guy. I rip my arms from Nick's neck and march the few steps to Rossi and his date, probably looking as crazy as everyone thinks I am, but I couldn't care less; I am livid.

"Are you serious?" I ask, right to his face.

"What?" He has the audacity to look confused. His date backs up. Smart girl.

"*Attention whore?* You think I tried to commit suicide for attention?" I'm pretty much yelling now, but I passed the point of caring about two minutes ago.

People gawk—what else is new?—and Rossi's eyes scan the crowd. He folds his arms in front of his chest. His face contorts into an ugly sneer, not like it was good to begin with.

He opens his mouth, but I'm done with the lies and whispers, and people drawing their own conclusions. Something breaks free inside of me. It's fierce and beautiful, and I feel it bubble over as the words fling like daggers from my mouth.

"I was raped, you jackass." He steps back in shock, arms dropping by his side.

My body deflates, most of the air draining out of me.

"I was raped," I say, quieter this time, "and you have no idea the scar that leaves on a person's soul. The shame. The guilt. You'll never know. So don't you dare presume to know me."

I turn, ready to storm away in my justified anger, but Nick stands there, arms open, waiting for me.

The room stops. The music fades. Time waits. And my strength cracks as the first tear drops. He gives me a smile, the one he never uses on anyone but me; and although I can't hear his voice over the sound of my pounding heart, I do catch the word "proud."

I close the remaining distance between us. And his arms enfold me. I grip the back of his shirt, crushing the white fabric. Needing to feel warmth. Needing to feel the grounding that only he can give me.

"So proud," he whispers into my ear.

Time picks back up and things come back into focus. Dani hovers behind Nick, close enough for me to see her tears. Her eyes lock with mine and right there and then I mourn the friendship we used to have before I moved here. I mourn all the secrets kept. All the anger, the bitterness, everything that was destroyed. She wipes her tears and then turns and walks away.

I take as deep a breath as I can. "Can we go?" I ask, feeling the stares of the room on us.

"Yeah."

He steps back and grabs my hand, giving it a squeeze.

We make our way through the crowd, people parting for us. I keep my head down until Nick stops. I look up and Regina stands in front of us. "You keep your head up," she says. "No more shame. No more hiding." Her eyes stay with mine. I nod once and we keep walking.

Craziest. Junior prom. Ever.

EPILOGUE

He strokes his thumb across my cheek as his hand pushes into the tangle of hair at the base of my neck. "Is this okay?" he asks.

I nod, too afraid to speak. Not sure if I want to push him away or keep going.

He leans in close and a tingle of unease snakes through my stomach. But he stops and stares into my eyes. Waiting. He's waiting for me to come the rest of the way.

I can do this.

He's not John.

I can do this.

I want to do this.

I lean into him, allowing his soft lips to brush mine. Only a whisper really. But a whisper of softness, strength, and the promise of better things to come.

I feel his lips pull into a smile against mine. Our lips brush each other again. Another soft caress. Just enough to lightly taste one another, but more than enough to flood my veins with fire.

He leans his forehead against mine. His breath, crisp and

minty, blows against my face. "You are the most amazing person, Victoria Adams. And I think I'm falling in love with you."

I didn't know joy could be something I could hold in the palm of my hand, but I feel it bolt from my fingertips and out my toes.

* * *

"I'm going to screw this up," I tell Dr. West.

"Probably," she agrees.

What's that? Oh, pretty sure that's my jaw. Sitting on the floor. "Wow, way to be supportive, Doc."

She lifts her hands as if to say, *hey, don't blame me.* "That's life, my dear. We all screw up; couldn't learn anything if we didn't. Just fix the screw-ups. Talk with him. Life isn't perfect and it never will be. We can have perfect moments, but we must work to be happy. You have to want it and always work toward it."

I study the scars on my wrists for a moment, finally uncovered for good, and then I look up into her face. "Am I going to be all right?"

She leans forward in her seat and reaches a hand across the desk for me to take. I do, and Dr. West squeezes it tight. "You've got this. You're not alone. Never. You can handle the ups, the downs, and the calm middles in between. It's time for you to live, Tori. Just live."

The End

A NOTE FROM THE AUTHOR

I might have started typing the words to this story eight years ago, but I lived parts of this book over fifteen years ago. Depression and anxiety are old friends that I wish would never come to visit. Suicide, depression, anxiety: they can be really hard to talk about, but I'm glad we can. I wanted to shine light on the thoughts and feelings a lot of us have had, so those that don't understand can see. And I wanted those who suffer like I have, to know they aren't alone, even when they feel like it. You've battled your worst day already; you can battle anything. We need you here. If you need help, or are thinking about suicide, call 800-273-8255 (and starting July of 2022, all you'll need to dial is 988) or visit https://suicidepre-ventionlifeline.org/

If you are a victim of sexual violence, I am so sorry. I am heartbroken that you had to experience that. And I want more than anything for you to get the help you need. Please call 800-656-4673 or visit https://www.rainn.org/

ACKNOWLEDGMENTS

I started this book eight years ago. Granted, there were a number of years I set it to the side so I could finish the Extraordinary Series, but it's been a long process. The amount of people that have helped me on this journey is enormous. And I'm sure to forget some people. I need to thank my dear friend and fellow author Katherine Cowley (check out her Mary Bennet series; they are amazing books). Thank you for looking at the book when I emailed you and said, "It's wrong, please help me fix it." Your continued support and friendship mean the world to me. Camille Fairbanks, I'm glad we're still friends after I roped you into editing this book. While I nearly cried at the amount of edits, I appreciate how thorough and helpful they were. Your advice has been crucial. Katie, Dena, Sara, Becky, Tara, Susan, and Cheryl—you ladies are gifts from God. I'm blessed to have you in my life and that you get the weird things about being an author. My writing groups Red Mountain and The Write Stuff—I'm eternally grateful for how you've helped me grow as a writer and have cheered me on throughout the years.

Thank you Jana for always schooling me on the dang comma.

But for real. Thank you for your help and willingness to make this better.

Something that has also helped while writing this book was music. The words of Birdy, Taylor Swift, Dashboard Confessional, The Strumbellas, Andy Grammer, Novo Amor, Vance Joy, and so many other artists have helped with my own creative flow. Your words are inspired and have deeply inspired me. Go listen to these artists if you haven't before.

Thank you to my amazing husband for being such a huge support in whatever endeavors I'm trying to tackle. Thank you to my kids who love that Mom writes books. Thank you to my parents who are my biggest cheerleaders. And finally, thank you to my readers for giving me a chance on what I consider a passion project.

ABOUT THE AUTHOR

Pam Eaton lives in the deserts of Arizona, but she'll always consider herself a New Englander at heart. She graduated from Arizona State University with degrees involving education and history. While she loves history, it'll always take a backseat to the fictional world she stumbled into as a young girl.

She lives with her husband, three kids, and two crazy but lovable labs. It's a chaotic life, but she wouldn't have it any other way. Especially since they let her read an insane amount of books, and watch way too many Food Network shows.

You can find out more at Pam's website
www.pameaton.com
peaton.ya@gmail.com

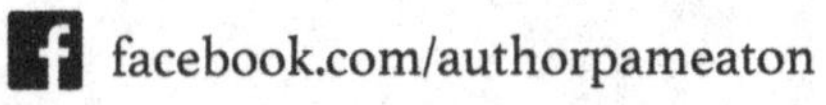

facebook.com/authorpameaton

instagram.com/author_pam_eaton

ALSO BY PAM EATON

The Extraordinary Series

An Extraordinary Few

The Blessed Many

An Army of One